Pokémon™ Adventures
FireRed & LeafGreen

Pokémon ADVENTURES
FireRed & LeafGreen
Volume 23
Perfect Square Edition

Story by HIDENORI KUSAKA
Art by SATOSHI YAMAMOTO

English Adaptation/Bryant Turnage
Translation/Tetsuichiro Miyaki
Touch-up & Lettering/Annaliese Christman
Design/Shawn Carrico
Editor/Annette Roman

Printed in the U.S.A.

Published by VIZ Media, LLC
P.O. Box 77010
San Francisco, CA 94107

10 9 8 7 6 5 4 3 2 1
First printing, July 2014

www.perfectsquare.com

www.viz.com

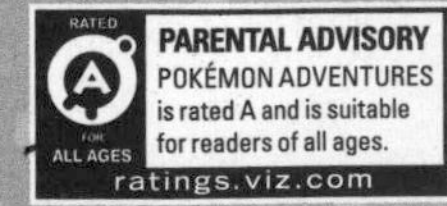

ratings.viz.com

23
VOLUME TWENTY
Hidenori Kusaka
Satoshi Yamamoto
POKÉMON™
ADVENTURES
FIRERED & LEAFGREEN

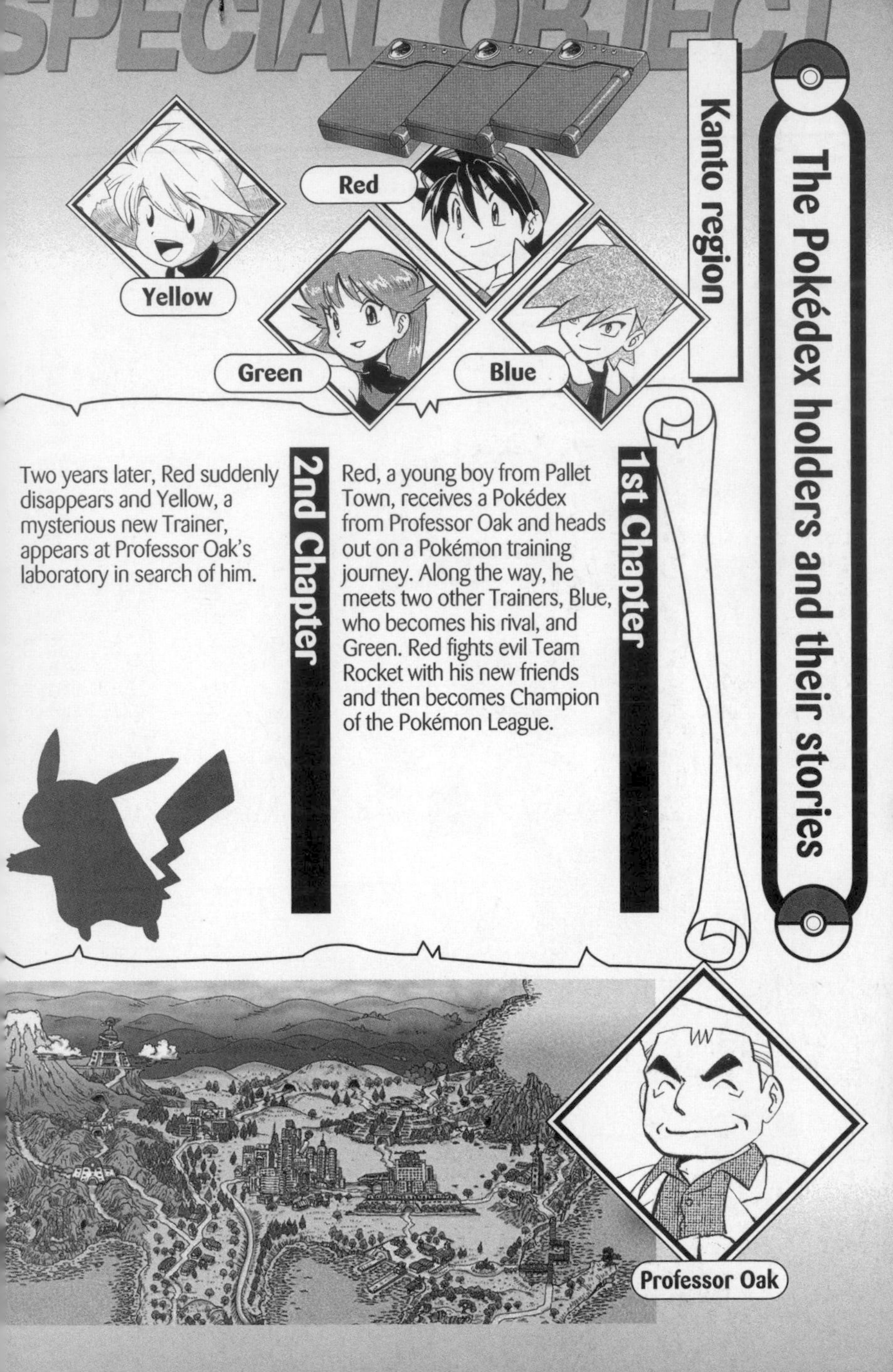
SPECIAL OBJECT
The Pokédex holders and their stories
Kanto region
Red
Yellow
Green
Blue
1st Chapter
Red, a young boy from Pallet Town, receives a Pokédex from Professor Oak and heads out on a Pokémon training journey. Along the way, he meets two other Trainers, Blue, who becomes his rival, and Green. Red fights evil Team Rocket with his new friends and then becomes Champion of the Pokémon League.
2nd Chapter
Two years later, Red suddenly disappears and Yellow, a mysterious new Trainer, appears at Professor Oak's laboratory in search of him.
Professor Oak

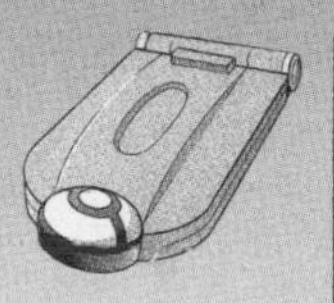

POKÉMON

Hoenn region

Jonto region

Gold

Crystal

Silver

4th Chapter

Pokémon Trainer Ruby has a passion for Pokémon Contests. He runs away from home right after his family moves to Littleroot Town. He meets a wild girl named Sapphire and they pledge to compete with each other in an 80-day challenge to...

3rd Chapter

A year later, Gold, a boy living in New Bark Town in a house full of Pokémon, sets out on a journey in pursuit of Silver, a Trainer who stole a Totodile from Professor Elm's laboratory. The two don't get along at first, but eventually they become partners fighting side by side. During their journey, they meet Crystal, the trainer who Professor Elm entrusts with the completion of his Pokédex. Together, the trio succeed to shatter the evil scheme of the Mask of Ice, a villain who leads what remains of Team Rocket.

Standing in Yellow's wa is the Kanto Elite Four, led by Lanc In a major battle at Cerise Islan Yellow manages to stymie th group's evil ambitions.

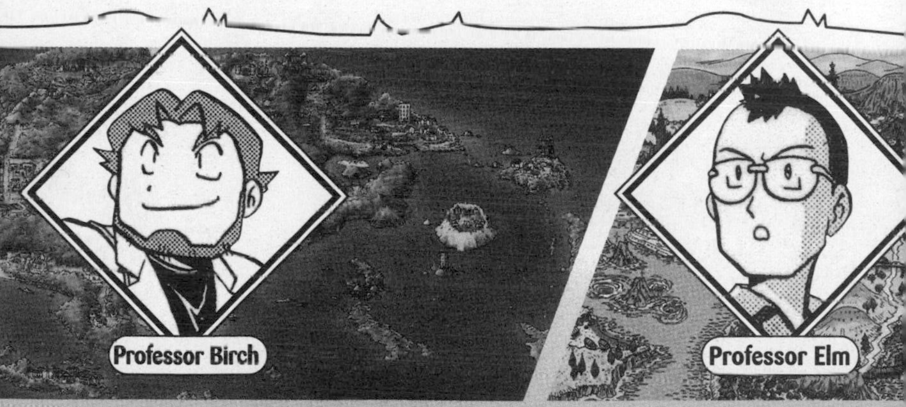

Kanto region
Red
Green
Blue
Sapphire
Ruby
...win every Pokémon Contest and every Pokémon Gym Battle, respectively. Meanwhile, in the Hoenn region, Team Aqua and Team Magma set their evil plot in motion. As a result, Legendary Pokémon Groudon and Kyogre are awakened and inflict catastrophic climate changes on Hoenn. In the end, thanks to Ruby and Sapphire's heroic efforts, the two legendary Pokémon go back into hibernation.
5th Chapter
Six months later, Red and Blue are called down to Professor Oak's laboratory, only to be attacked by a mysterious enemy. They then discover messages from Professor Oak instructing them to give up their Pokédexes...

POKÉMON™ ADVENTURES FIRERED & LEAFGREEN

CONTENTS

FIRE RED
LEAF GREEN

The Fifth Chapter

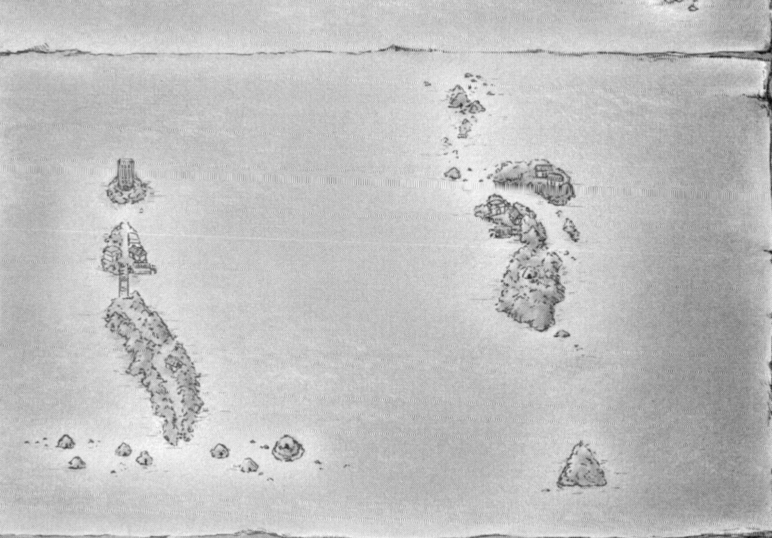

• Adventure 268 •
The Escape

FLASH
WE HAVE A BREAK-OUT!

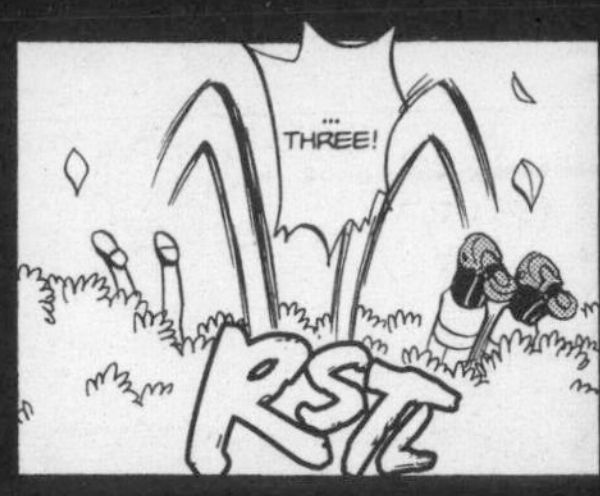

SO **THAT'S** WHAT YOU LOOK LIKE!

COME ON. WE'VE GOT TO HURRY UP AND GET OUT OF HERE—**NOW**!

THREE PAIRS OF BOYS AND GIRLS WERE CHOSEN TO BE THE "MASKED CHILDREN"...AND TRAINED TO BE THE "ARMS AND LEGS" OF THE MASK OF ICE.

WE WERE KIDNAPPED BY HO-OH WHEN WE WERE VERY YOUNG.

THIS IS WHERE WE ARE NOW.
LET'S DO A QUICK DOUBLE-CHECK, SILVER...
BUT GREEN AND I HAVE ALWAYS LOOKED FOR AN OPPORTUNITY TO ESCAPE.
WE MANAGED TO GET OUT OF THE BUILDING WHERE WE'VE BEEN LIVING AND TRAINING ALL THIS TIME...
BUT THE WHOLE AREA IS SURROUNDED BY A FORCE FIELD CREATED BY PSYCHIC-TYPE POKÉMON.
AND THE ONLY WAY TO GET PAST IT IS...
SCRCH
... THROUGH ...
...THIS UNDER-GROUND PASSAGE. IT'S THE ONLY WAY OUTSIDE.
IT WAS TOO HARD FOR ME TO FULLY INVESTIGATE THE ROUTE LEADING OUTSIDE IN ADVANCE.
BUT THAT'S ALL I KNOW...
KLANK
KLANK
KLANK

HEY! THEY WENT THAT-A-WAY!
OVER THERE!
DON'T LET THEM ESCAPE!
OVER HERE!
PLUS ...
...HIS ROOM IS SOMEWHERE BETWEEN HERE AND THE EXIT!
TMP
DON'T LET THEM SEE YOUR FACE!
THERE THEY ARE!
!
EEVEE, BITE!
NATU, PSYCHIC!
HOUNDOUR, EMBER!
MEOWTH, SCRATCH!

SMASH
WHOA!
FSSSS
SILVER!
SCRATCH
DON'T WORRY! I SAW WHICH WAY THEY WENT!
FSSS
KOFF KOFF!
WHOA!

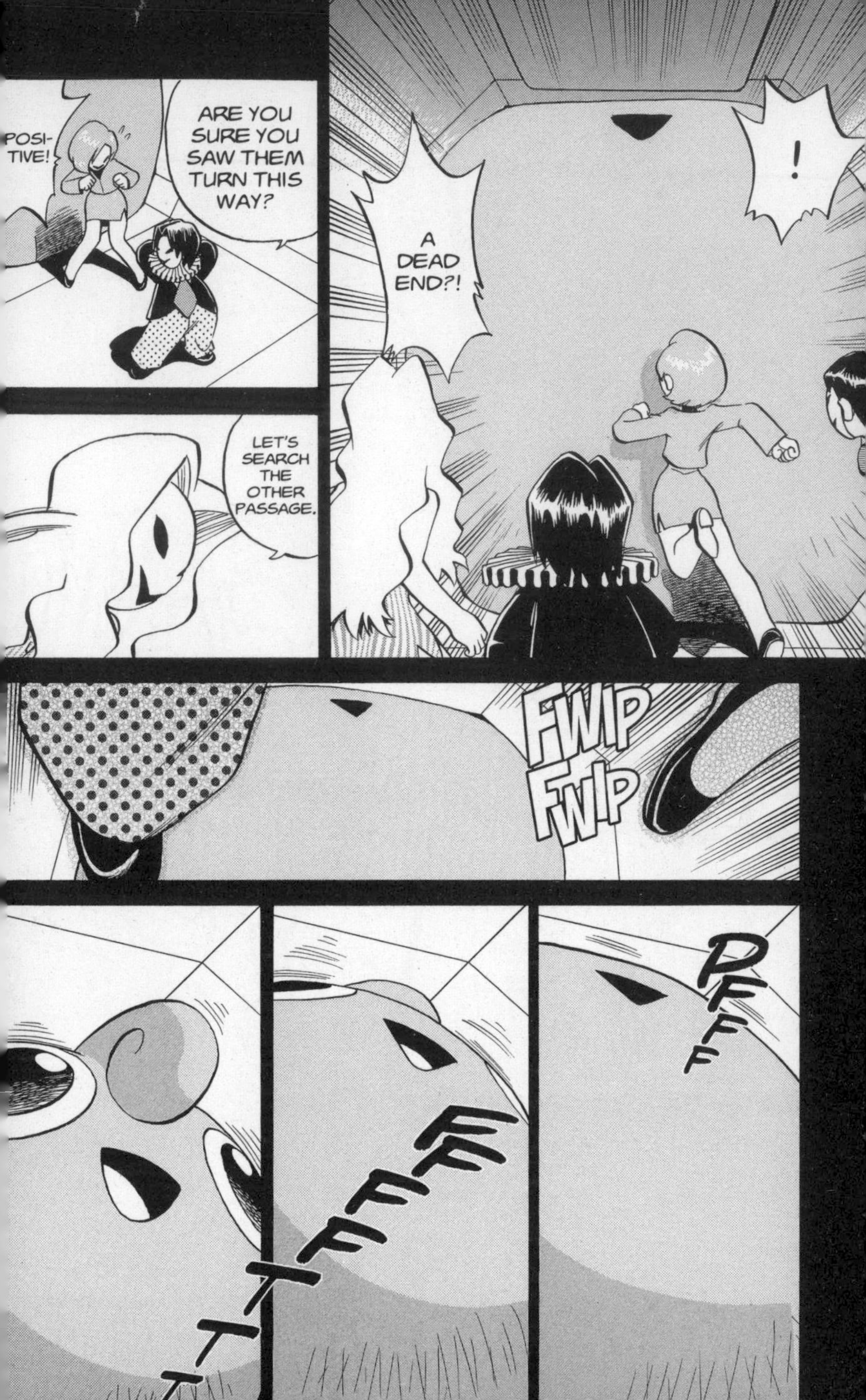
ARE YOU SURE YOU SAW THEM TURN THIS WAY?
POSI-TIVE!
LET'S SEARCH THE OTHER PASSAGE.
!
A DEAD END?!
FWIP FWIP
PFFFF
FFFFTTTT

WE DON'T NEED TO WORRY ABOUT ANYBODY ELSE COMING AFTER US.
FFFTTTT
THE EXIT MUST BE NEARBY.
!!
WHOA!
THIS MUST BE HIS ROOM.
IT'S GOT A CARVING OF US ON IT!!
THAT WAS A SURPRISE! IT'S ALL RIGHT, THOUGH. JUST A STATUE.
CAREFUL, GREEN... WE DON'T KNOW WHERE HE IS! HE COULD BE IN THERE RIGHT NOW!
THAT'S RIGHT. AND HE IS IN THERE, ACTU-ALLY.
HE'S SLEEPING ON THE OTHER SIDE OF THAT CURTAIN.
WHAT ?!

DON'T WORRY. HE CAN BARELY MOVE TODAY.
THERE'S A DAY ONCE EVERY FEW MONTHS WHEN HE GETS REALLY WEAK FOR SOME REASON.
AND IF MY CALCULATIONS ARE CORRECT, THAT DAY IS... ...TODAY!
GREEN WAS RIGHT.
LATER, WE FOUND OUT THAT AT THAT POINT THE MASK OF ICE HAD ALREADY TRIED TO TRAVEL THROUGH TIME.
A LIGHT WOULD SHINE DOWN ON THE ILEX FOREST SHRINE WHEN THE MOON WAS WAXING OR WANING.
HE DIDN'T KNOW ABOUT THE POKÉ BALL THAT CAN CAPTURE TIME, SO HE WOULD TRY TO CATCH THE LIGHT WITHOUT IT. AND EVERY TIME HE WOULD GET HURT.
IT'S NOT ENOUGH TO ESCAPE WITH JUST THE CLOTHES ON OUR BACKS...
HMM...
HEH HEH...
LET'S TAKE THESE WITH US TOO!
FWIP

I CAN SEE IT!
FWIP
THERE IT IS!
ZOOM
THE WORLD OUTSIDE!
HUF. HUF.
THEY'VE ...
... ESCAPED ...
TINK
TINK
TINK
TINK
...
IMPOSSIBLE!

THAT'S...AN EMOTION. I THOUGHT I'D RID MYSELF OF THOSE... LONG AGO...

WHAT'S THIS I FEEL...? LONELI-NESS?

GREEN AND I MANAGED TO SURVIVE ON OUR OWN, BUT THE MEMORIES OF THAT MAN LEFT A SHADOW ON US...

AND THAT WAS THE FIRST DAY OF THE REST OF OUR LIVES—OF FREEDOM ON THE OUTSIDE!

THERE WAS A THORN THAT REMAINED STUCK IN HER HEART.

A NICKNAME FOR YOUR POKÉMON?! IT DOESN'T NEED ONE!

FOR SOME REASON, SHE NICKNAMED ALL HER POKÉMON EXCEPT JIGGLYPUFF, HER OLDEST PARTNER.

BUT AFTER A WHILE, I BEGAN TO NOTICE CHANGES IN HER...
I FOUND OUT WHY... IT WAS BECAUSE SHE HAD MET OTHER POKÉDEX HOLDERS.
JIGGLY Lv.53
EXP. / 119101
NEXT 6870 TO LV54
No. 039
SING PP 15/15
DOUBLE-EDGE PP 15/15
DOUBLE SLAP PP 10/10
DEFENSE CURL PP 40/40
AND NOW...
TODAY'S THE DAY, GREEN...

HEH. YEAH. I'M A LITTLE NERVOUS...
I CAN'T BELIEVE I'M FINALLY GOING TO SEE MY MOM AND DAD AGAIN!

I HEARD THEY'VE BEEN TRAVEL-ING THE WORLD IN SEARCH OF YOU.
UH-HUH... AND WE FINALLY GOT IN TOUCH WITH EACH OTHER ...

... I'M SORRY, SILVER ...
IT'S OKAY, GREEN.

YOU'VE BEEN LOOKING AFTER ME ALL THIS TIME, EVEN THOUGH YOU DON'T KNOW WHO I AM OR WHERE I'M FROM—NOT EVEN MY BIRTHDAY.
DON'T WORRY ABOUT ME.
SILVER ...

DID YOU GET THE HAT AND DRESS I SENT? I THOUGHT YOU'D LIKE TO WEAR THEM FOR THIS SPECIAL DAY.

TALK TO YOU LATER.

WELL...

I DID! AND I LOVE THEM!

THANKS, SILVER!

BUT... DO YOU THINK A FANCY OUTFIT LIKE THIS...

...SUITS ME?

OF COURSE IT DOES.

I HAD NO IDEA THAT...

...THIS WAS GOING TO BE...

WELL, SNEASEL... WE'D BETTER...

...GET GOING TOO...

SILVE

FLAP FLAP

IT'S BEEN ABOUT SIX MONTHS...
...SINCE THAT FIERCE BATTLE BETWEEN KYOGRE AND GROUDON...

• Adventure 269 •
Return to Pallet Town

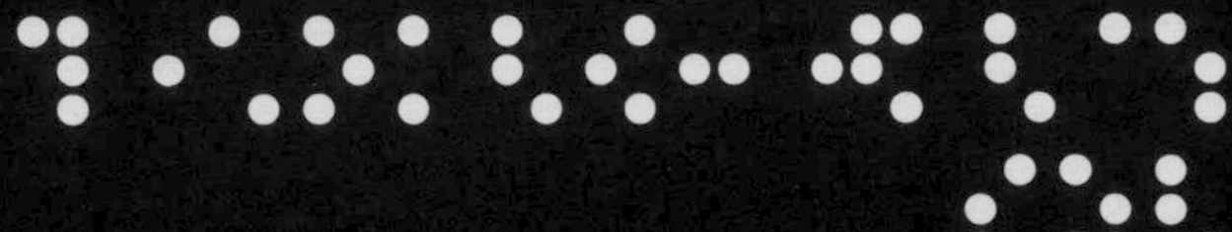

POKÉMON
ADVENTURES
FIRERED & LEAFGREEN
The Fifth Chapter

I'M GONNA CAPTURE THIS NIDORINO AND TRAIN IT!

OH YEAH!

HUH?

BOINK

HMPH... I FAILED...

HA HA HA! THAT'S BECAUSE YOU THREW THE POKÉ BALL FIRST.

YOU HAVE TO **FIGHT** THE POKÉMON **BEFORE** YOU TRY TO CATCH IT.

HEY, IT LOOKS LIKE YOU HAVE A POWERFUL GENGAR!

BRING IT OUT TO FIGHT FOR YOU—COME ON!

WHAT? OH, OKAY.

BOOM
UM, EXCUSE ME, BUT... ARE YOU TWO...?
HURRY UP NOW! WE NEED TO GET GOING ...
SMASH
SEE? THIS TIME YOU DIDN'T FAIL!

PALLET TOWN HASN'T CHANGED A BIT...
SEEMS LIKE FOREVER SINCE WE'VE BEEN BACK...
DID YOU NOTICE...? THOSE KIDS ARE JUST LIKE US BEFORE WE GOT OUR POKÉDEXES!
HA! YOU'RE RIGHT!

PROFESSOR OAK—YOUR GRANDPA—WENT TO CHECK ON THE HOENN REGION AFTER THE BIG BATTLE THERE, BUT HE SHOULD BE BACK BY NOW.
RED
A POKÉDEX HOLDER WHO WON THE INDIGO PLATEAU POKÉMON LEAGUE.

YEAH. AND HE'S EXPECTING US.
BLUE
ALSO A POKÉDEX HOLDER, AND THE GRANDSON OF RENOWNED POKÉMON RESEARCHER PROFESSOR OAK.

DON'T WANT TO KEEP HIM WAITING!
BUT YOU KEEP GETTING SIDE-TRACKED, RED!
OAK POKÉMON RESEARCH LABORATORY
HEH HEH...

SQUEEK
LONG TIME NO SEE, PROFES-SOR OAK!
PROFES-SOR?!

STRANGE, HE DOESN'T SEEM TO BE HOME.
HUH ?!

To BLUE
To RED
To GREEN

WHAT'S THIS? THERE'S ONE FOR YOU AND ME, BLUE.

GREEN

HMM... IT'S AN ENVE-LOPE ...

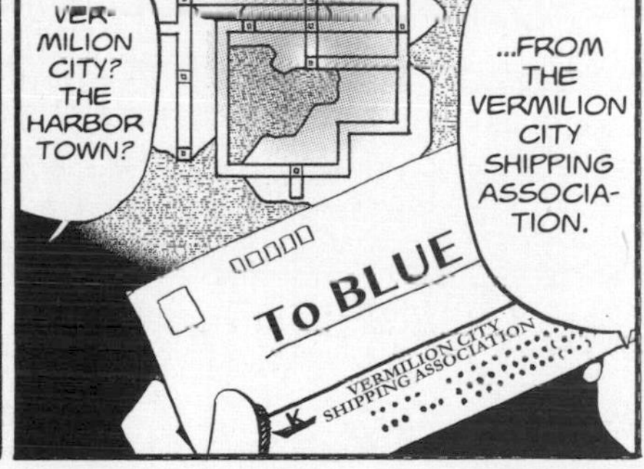
...FROM THE VERMILION CITY SHIPPING ASSOCIA-TION.
VER-MILION CITY? THE HARBOR TOWN?
To BLUE
VERMILION CITY SHIPPING ASSOCIATION

SO MAYBE THE REASON HE WANTED TO SEE US HAS SOMETHING TO DO WITH VERMILION CITY...?
I GUESS WE'LL FIND OUT AS SOON AS WE LOOK INSIDE...
RRIP

KRASH

ZIP
WHAT?!
SWISH
SAUR!
THUD
SMASH
CHARIZARD!
SLASH
SMAK
WHAT'S GOING ON? WHAT ARE THEY FIGHTING AGAINST—?!
WHATEVER IT IS, IT'S TOO QUICK!

FWOOSH
CHARIZARD, FLAMETHROWER!
SAUR, SOLARBEAM!
PFFEW
FWAMF
SSSSS
HUF
HUF
HUF
RSTL
WHAT ARE YOU DOING, RED?!
ZZIP
WHATEVER THAT WAS, WE NEED TO TALK TO PROFESSOR OAK—AND FAST!
WHY ISN'T HE HERE ANYWAY? HE CALLED US ALL THE WAY OUT HERE TO MEET WITH HIM!
I'M GOING TO GO LOOK FOR HIM!

DEAR POKÉDEX HOLDERS, LISTEN CAREFULLY. I'M GOING TO HAVE TO...

...TAKE AWAY YOUR POKÉDEXES !!

• Adventure 270 •
Now You See Me...

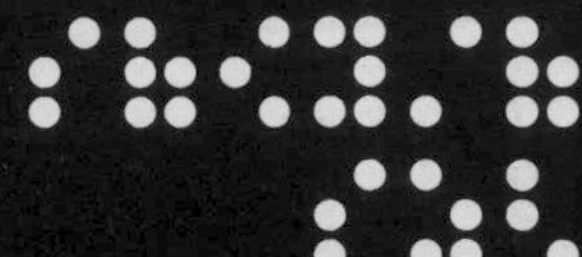

Pokémon Adventures
FireRed & LeafGreen
The Fifth Chapter

DEAR POKÉDEX HOLDERS, LISTEN CAREFULLY. I'M GOING TO HAVE TO...
...TAKE AWAY YOUR POKÉDEXES!

THE COMPUTER ON MY DESK IS CONNECTED TO THE STORAGE SYSTEM.
I WANT YOU TO PLACE YOUR POKÉDEXES IN THERE.

NO MATTER HOW MANY TIMES I LISTEN TO IT, IT'S THE SAME... THIS MESSAGE FROM PROFESSOR OAK...
...RECORDED ON THIS FAME CHECKER WITH MY NAME ON IT...
...
BLUE!

KLICK
KLICK
KLICK
FSSSSST
TINK
STRTCH

...

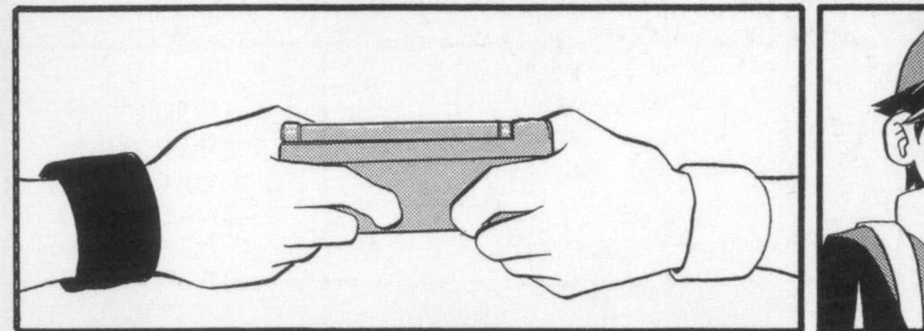

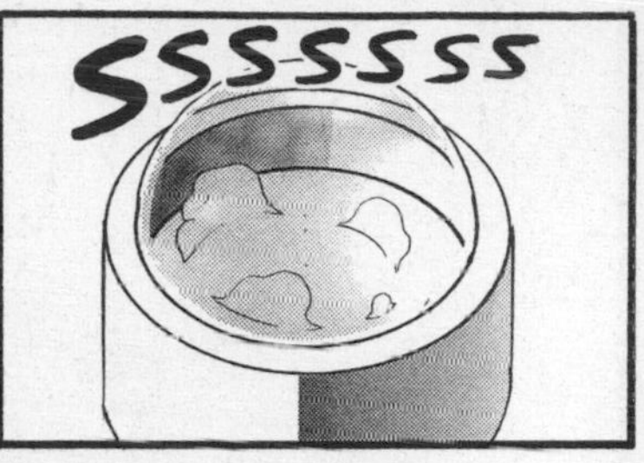
SSSSSSS

OUR POKÉ-DEXES ...
...ARE GONE.

IF THAT'S WHAT PROFESSOR OAK WANTS, THAT'S WHAT HE GETS!
RIGHT. SAME GOES FOR ME.

I HAVE NO IDEA WHY HE DECIDED TO TAKE THE POKÉDEXES AWAY FROM US...
BUT...

BOM
AERO!

LET'S GO, BLUE! TO VER-MILION CITY!

YEAH!

YOINK
TO GREEN
CATCH
FLAPFLAP
VERMILION CITY
EH?

YOU'RE AWFULLY EARLY.
THE SHIP WON'T BE LAUNCHING FOR SOME TIME, YOU KNOW.
WHY ARE YOU HERE ALREADY...?
I'M GOING TO MEET MY FATHER AND MOTHER.
I HAVEN'T SEEN THEM FOR A VERY LONG TIME.
I SEE. NO WONDER YOU LOOK SO EXCITED.
OKAY THEN... IN THAT CASE...
WHY DON'T YOU GET ON BOARD NOW...?
IT'LL BE MORE FUN TO WAIT ON THE SHIP, WON'T IT?
REALLY? OKAY!
Plus, you're kinda cute!

DO YOU HAVE YOUR TRI-PASS WITH YOU?
YES!
Tri-Pass

OH? WAIT A SEC... I HAVEN'T CONNECTED THE GANG-PLANK TO THE SHIP YET!
NO PROB-LEM!
BLASTY!
BOM
!

LET'S GO!

FOOSH
OOOH!

TNKTNKTNK

TMP

I'LL TAKE A LOOK AROUND THE SHIP WHILE I WAIT...

THANK YOU SO MUCH!

HEY!

GREEN

POKÉMON TRAINER. THIRD PLACE WINNER AT THE POKÉMON LEAGUE.

OOOOSH

SHE FINISHED IN THE TOP RANKS AT THE POKÉMON LEAGUE—THE ONE BEFORE LAST!

SHE'S THE ONE PROFESSOR OAK GAVE THE POKÉ-DEX TO!

I **THOUGHT** I'D SEEN THAT GIRL SOME-WHERE BEFORE!

WHAT A LUXURIOUS SHIP!
TOSS
YOU SHOULD ALL GET TO EXPLORE IT...

GO FOR IT!

FLOOP FLOOP
WHAT'S WRONG, DITTY?
STRCCCCH
SHAKE SHAKE

ZING
SOME-THING'S HERE...!

KRRASSH

FWIP FWIP FWIP

AH!

BLASTY!

EVERYONE!

WHOA!

FWUMP

LET'S GO!

JUMP

YOU CAUGHT ME BY SURPRISE!

OH ...?

ARE YOU BOARDING THE *SEAGALLOP* AS WELL?!

Tri-Pass

Tri-Pass

YOU'RE HOLDING A TRI-PASS!

SOME PASSENGERS ARRIVE TOO EARLY AND SOME PASSENGERS ARRIVE TOO LATE—ALMOST!
EH?
FWOOOT
PHEW, YOU MADE IT.
IT'S ABOUT TO DEPART ANY MINUTE NOW!
GET ON BOARD! GET ON BOARD!

YOU WOULDN'T HAPPEN TO BE...
...POKÉDEX HOLDERS...WHO RECEIVED YOUR POKÉDEXES FROM PRO-FESSOR OAK, WOULD YOU?!
Well, yes... Sort of...

RM M
WOW, I'VE MET SO MANY CELEB-RITIES TODAY!
RMMRMM

CALLING ALL PASSEN-GERS!

RMBL RMBL

THE *SEAGALLOP* IS NOW DEPARTING FROM VERMILION CITY HARBOR!

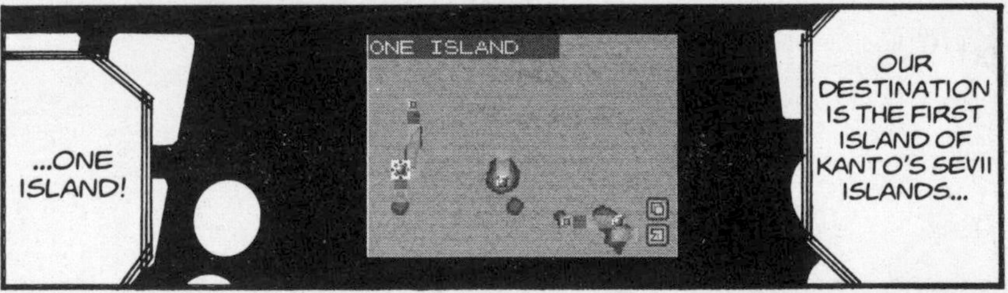

OUR DESTINATION IS THE FIRST ISLAND OF KANTO'S SEVII ISLANDS...
ONE ISLAND
...ONE ISLAND!

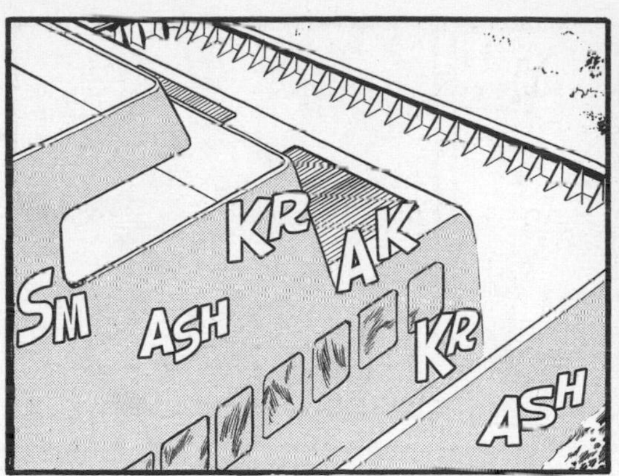

FIRST, I HAVE TO FIGURE OUT WHAT I'M FIGHTING AGAINST!

SMASH

AH!

THEN I'LL USE ...
... THIS!

SHOOT! I DON'T HAVE MY POKÉDEX!

THE SILPH SCOPE...
...WHICH LETS ME SEE GHOSTS!
SNAP

SMASH
I'VE IMPROVED IT SO IT CAN IDENTIFY ANY POKÉMON!
NOW ...
...SHOW YOUR-SELF!

WNZZZ
GRAB
SLAP
AH ...!
THAT'S ...!

URGH ...
I CAN'T BREATHE... OR MOVE!
ZOOP
!
SQU EEZE
I'M BEING STRANGLED BY...SOME KIND OF INVISIBLE FORCE...
FFP
MY SILPH SCOPE ...
FFF
P
F
SNAP
FP
...GOT DRAGGED INTO THAT... DARK- NESS!

HM...

WE GOT ON WITHOUT A CLUE AS TO WHERE WE'RE GOING...

WHAT KIND OF PLACE IS THIS ONE ISLAND ANYWAY?

A I Y E E E!
ZZZTZZZZTZZT
I'VE SEEN THAT THERE PIKACHU BEFORE!
ARE YA...
YEP! THIS ELECTRIC SHOCK! I KNEW IT...
PIKA!
DOES THAT MEAN ...!
BILL!
RED! BLUE!
IS DAISY...
...HERE TOO?
NOPE.
SHE STAYED BEHIND.
LONG TIME NO SEE!
HOW'S IT GOIN' ?!

NEVER IMAGINED I'D RUN INTO Y'ALL ON THE *SEAGALLOP*.
WHAT BRINGS YA'LL TO ONE ISLAND? VACATION?
NO... UMM...
IT SURE IS A NICE PLACE! IF I DIDN'T HAFTA WORK, I'D—
YOU'RE GOING THERE FOR WORK?
YUP. I'M HEADIN' DOWN TO MEET CELIO—A RESEARCHER BUDDY OF MINE. GONNA HELP 'IM TWEAK HIS TRANSPORTER.

I DEVELOPED THE POKÉMON TRANSPORTER AND STORAGE SYSTEM WITH SOME PALS...

THEY'RE SPREAD OUT ALL OVER NOW. CELIO'S ONE OF 'EM.

HE'S IN CHARGE OF MANAGIN' THE SYSTEM AT SEVII ISLANDS.

BRIGETTE

LANETTE

CELIO

SEVII ISLANDS?

WHAT? DON'TCHA KNOW?

IT'S AN ARCHIPELAGO MADE UP OF SEVEN ISLANDS. ONE ISLAND IS JUST ONE OF THEM.

OH, HOLD ON A MINUTE.

SPEAKIN' OF TROUBLE, IT'S CELIO!

BRRING

HIYA! BILL SPEAKIN'!

I'LL BE THEAH SHORTLY. HOW'S IT GOIN' IN YOUR NECK OF TH' WOODS?

NOTHING'S CHANGED. I STILL CAN'T CONNECT TO THE STORAGE SYSTEM.
AS A MATTER OF FACT, IT'S GOTTEN WORSE.
AT FIRST WE JUST HAD TROUBLE CONNECTING TO THE KANTO MAINLAND...
...BUT NOW WE CAN'T EVEN CONNECT TO THE OTHER ISLANDS OF SEVII.

I CAN'T FIGURE OUT WHY THIS IS HAPPENING!
WELL, I'LL TAKE A LOOK-SEE WHEN I GET THEAH. MEET ME AT THE NETWORK CENTER, ALL RIGHT?

DING
DONG
HMPH... WHAT A PAIN.

CALLING ALL PASSENGERS... THANK YOU FOR SAILING WITH THE *SEAGALLOP*...

WE ARE NOW DOCKING AT ONE ISLAND...

SQUEEZE
URGH...

THE SHIP HAS ARRIVED. BUT I CAN'T LET...
...THIS INVISIBLE OPPONENT... GET ONTO THAT ISLAND!

I HAVE TO...WARN SOMEBODY ABOUT THIS...

OH...! DAD! MOM!

THEY'RE LOOKING AT MY PHOTO-GRAPH! THEY'VE SEEN ME...

NO ...

THEY'RE COMING THIS WAY!

ISN'T THAT GREEN ?!
HEY ...

THE DARK-NESS ...
FF
F
IT'S GOING TO....
FF

SOME-THING'S WRONG!
WE'VE GOT TO HELP HER!
FWIP FWIP

DAD! MOM! NO-O-O-O!
STOP!
ZLIP
ZOOOP
ZOOP
ZOOOP

ZOOOP
TNK
FSSS
BLIP
WHY...?
DAD! MOM!
WHY ?!

CHARACTER PROFILE RED

RED

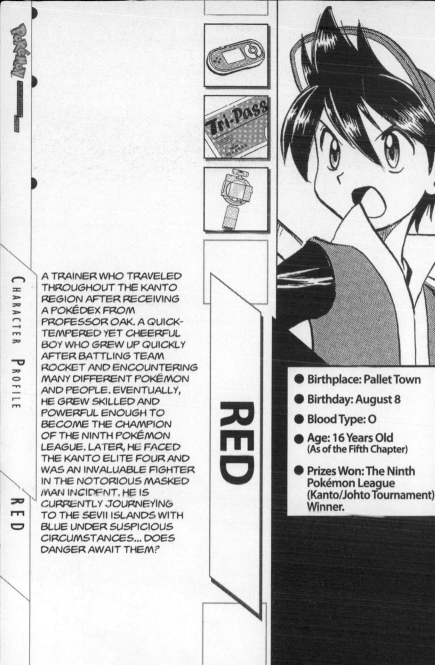

A TRAINER WHO TRAVELED THROUGHOUT THE KANTO REGION AFTER RECEIVING A POKÉDEX FROM PROFESSOR OAK. A QUICK-TEMPERED YET CHEERFUL BOY WHO GREW UP QUICKLY AFTER BATTLING TEAM ROCKET AND ENCOUNTERING MANY DIFFERENT POKÉMON AND PEOPLE. EVENTUALLY, HE GREW SKILLED AND POWERFUL ENOUGH TO BECOME THE CHAMPION OF THE NINTH POKÉMON LEAGUE. LATER, HE FACED THE KANTO ELITE FOUR AND WAS AN INVALUABLE FIGHTER IN THE NOTORIOUS MASKED MAN INCIDENT. HE IS CURRENTLY JOURNEYING TO THE SEVII ISLANDS WITH BLUE UNDER SUSPICIOUS CIRCUMSTANCES... DOES DANGER AWAIT THEM?

- **Birthplace: Pallet Town**
- **Birthday: August 8**
- **Blood Type: O**
- **Age: 16 Years Old** (As of the Fifth Chapter)
- **Prizes Won: The Ninth Pokémon League (Kanto/Johto Tournament) Winner.**

• Adventure 271 •
...Now You Don't.

WHY...?
GREEN?!
DAD... MOM...
GTGGR
HOW COULD THIS HAPPEN ...?
HWOOSH
NO!
TOSS
POLI, GO!
BOOM

GRAB
TMP
NICE WORK, POLI!
IS THE ENEMY ...
...STILL NEARBY ...?
SCIZOR!
BOM

KRN
CAPTURE THE INVISIBLE ENEMY...
GRAB
!
HIT IT!
OP

HSSSSS

BLUE! WE HAVE TO TAKE HER TO A HOSPI-TAL!

WHATEVER YOU WERE FIGHTING... IS GONE NOW...

...
JINGLE JINGLE

...
__Month __Day
I finally get to meet my Mom and Dad tomorrow!

A FEW HOURS LATER...

POKÉMON NET CENTER

WE'RE MIGHTY THANKFUL, CELIO.

WE DON'T KNOW ANYTHING 'BOUT THIS ISLAND... GLAD YOU WERE HERE T' HELP.

NO PROBLEM, BILL. I'M JUST GLAD THERE WAS A BED FREE AT THE FIRST AID STATION.

AND THOSE POOR POKÉMON...
HER BLASTOISE AND THE OTHERS ARE BEING TREATED RIGHT NOW AS WELL.
APPARENTLY THEIR TRAINER...
...HAS BEEN TRAUMATIZED BY THIS INCIDENT...
THAT'S WHAT THE DOCTOR SAID.

WELL... I'LL BE GOING THEN...
SURE THING. AND... THANKS.
BILL, ARE YOU SURE THAT...
...GREEN CAME TO THIS ISLAND TO MEET HER FATHER AND MOTHER?
NO DOUBT ABOUT IT.
I WAS SORRY TA DO IT, BUT... AH READ HER DIARY. FOUND IT ON THE FLOOR.

YEP...
HARD TA BELIEVE, HUH?

THAT MEANS THOSE PEOPLE WHO DISAP-PEARED ...
...MUST HAVE BEEN GREEN'S PARENTS.

_Month __Day
finally get to meet my Mom and Dad tomorrow!

THE IMPORTANT THING NOW IS TA FIND OUT WHAT HAPPENED TO 'EM.

YOU CAIN'T HELP BUT FEEL SORRY FOR HER.
GRAB

WHAT ?!
ACCORDIN' TO HER DIARY, GREEN WAS AT PALLET TOWN YESTERDAY.

HURMM.
FLIP FLIP

!
AND... IT SAYS HERE SHE...
...RETURNED HER POKÉDEX TO PROFES-SOR OAK.

SHE RETURNED HER POKÉDEX TO PROFESSOR OAK AND...SHE WAS ATTACKED BY A MYSTERIOUS ENEMY!
FWIP
RRASSH
SWISH
AH!
JUST LIKE US!

GRR
RIGHT. THIS IS NO COINCIDENCE.
IT'S A GOOD THING YOU RETRIEVED HER DIARY.

BUT I'VE FOUND ...
... SOMETHING EVEN BETTER.

GREEN'S SILPH SCOPE!

IT'S BADLY DAMAGED, BUT THE PLAYBACK FUNCTION STILL WORKS.
SHE MUST HAVE BEEN WEARING IT WHEN SHE WAS FIGHTING THAT INVISIBLE ENEMY.

RSSSP
THIS SCOPE SHOULD TELL US SOMETHING ...!

!

WHAT TH' HECK IS THAT...?!

BLUE AND I ARE GOING TO FIGHT THIS ENEMY!

AND...

...WE'LL DEFEAT IT...

...NO MATTER WHAT!

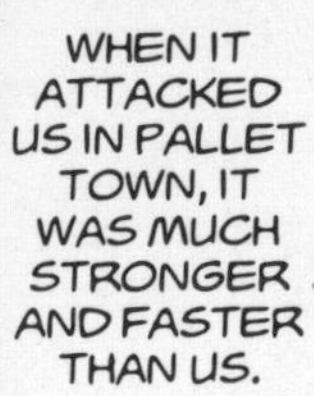

THEN WHAT ARE YA FIXIN' TA DO?!
WE'LL JUST HAVE TO TRAIN AND IMPROVE OUR SKILLS THEN!

THAT ...
... DOESN'T MAKE ANY SENSE ...

I HAVEN'T MET ANY TRAINERS STRONGER'N YOU TWO IN THE LAST FIVE YEARS!
HOW ARE YA GONNA IMPROVE YOUR SKILLS WHEN YOU'RE ALREADY SO STRONG? ARE YA PULLIN' MAH LEG?!
WHAT ARE YA THINKIN' ?!

WE HAVE TO.

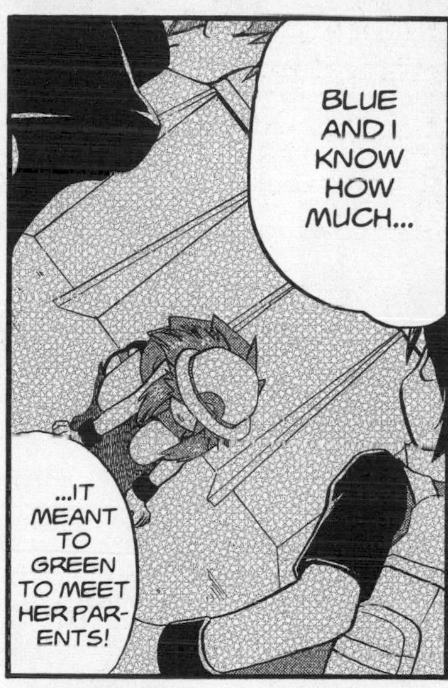
BLUE AND I KNOW HOW MUCH...
...IT MEANT TO GREEN TO MEET HER PAR-ENTS!

SHE LOST THEM FOR THE SECOND TIME— RIGHT IN FRONT OF US! THAT'S MORE THAN ENOUGH REASON FOR US TO FIGHT!

...

BUT WE DON'T HAVE A LOT OF TIME TO TRAIN...
HOW ARE WE GOING TO IMPROVE OUR SKILLS IN SUCH A SHORT TIME...?
HM ...

THERE IS ONE WAY FOR YOU TO BECOME STRONGER.
PEOPLE SAY "FRIENDS GATHER AT KNOT ISLAND"...
AND THIS LOOKS LIKE AN INTERESTING FRIENDSHIP RIGHT HERE.
JINGLE
I HAD A PREMONITION THAT...
...YOU TWO MIGHT COME HERE TO MASTER ...
CACKLE CACKLE
...MY...
...SPECIAL MOVES!
JINGLE JINGLE

POKÉMON ON TEAM RED 1

Pika/Pikachu ♂

Electric

- **LV. 88** (As of Adventure 271)
- **Ability: Static**
- **Sassy Nature**

Pika met Red at Pewter City and since then has been a core member of Red's team. When Red went missing, Pika traveled with Yellow.

Poli/Poliwrath ♂

Water
Fighting

- **LV. 80** (As of Adventure 271)
- **Ability: Damp**
- **Brave Nature**

Poli is the first Pokémon Red caught as a child. Poli has fought alongside Red for a long time and is great backup for the team.

Saur/Venusaur ♂

Grass
Poison

- **LV. 82** (As of Adventure 271)
- **Ability: Overgrow**
- **Gentle Nature**

Red received this Pokémon with the Pokédex from Professor Oak. Saur has evolved into its final form after countless adventures.

• Adventure 272 •
Old Ultima Puts Them to the Test

I HAD A PREMONITION! A PREMONITION THAT YOU TWO MIGHT BE ABLE TO MASTER...
...MY SPECIAL MOVE!
...
HEY, WE'RE KIND OF IN A HURRY, GRANDMA. WE DON'T HAVE TIME TO CHAT.
WHAT?!
COME BACK HERE, YOU WHIPPER-SNAPPERS!
SWISH

WZZZZZZ
CHARIZARD!
SAUR!
BOOM
WFF WFF WFF
WAP

KA-CHING

BFFF

...POKÉMON TRAINERS... USE YOUR POKÉMON ...

BOOM

...AND SHOW ME THE STUFF YOU'RE MADE OF!

FOOOSH
LET'S HEAR THE RUMBLE OF BATTLE! THE CRACKLE OF BLAZING FIRE!
PULL IT OUT! THE POWER OF VERDURE!
ROOARRR
KRASH

URK!
Oops ...
ACK!

!
TIME TO PREPARE FOR DEPARTURE ...

ER, SORRY. GOT CARRIED AWAY. PUT A LITTLE TOO MUCH OOMPH INTO THAT, HEH HEH...
ULTIMA! YOU AGAIN!?

ALL RIGHT, ALREADY... BUT SHOULDN'T YOU BE MORE RESPECTFUL OF YOUR FRAGILE ELDERS...?
UNDER-STOOD, ULTIMA ?!
!
"ULTIMA" ?

OH CRIMINEY! I ONLY LET YOU ONBOARD BECAUSE YOU SAID YOU WERE JUST GOING SIGHTSEEING AT KINDLE ROAD AND MT. EMBER.
IF YOU'RE GOING TO CAUSE A RUCKUS AS USUAL, I'M TAKING YOU RIGHT BACK TO TWO ISLAND!

YOU KNOW HER, BILL?
ULTIMA... ULTIMA...

I'VE HEARD THAT NAME SOMEWHERE BEFORE... BACK WHEN I WAS JUST A YOUNG'UN.
A STORY 'BOUT AN OLD LADY... WHO LIVES ALONE ON A FAR-OFF ISLAND NEAR THE KANTO MAINLAND... WHERE SHE SAFE-GUARDS THE TRADITION OF SPECIAL POKÉMON MOVES.
AND THAT OLD LADY'S MONIKER IS...
...ULTI-MA!

OOH, I'M GLAD TO SEE MY FAME PRECEDES ME—WITH SOMEONE AT LEAST.
THAT'S ME ALL RIGHT!

A GUARD-IAN OF... SPECIAL MOVES?!
SHE MIGHT BE AMAZING, BUT... THAT DOESN'T GIVE HER THE RIGHT TO SLAP THESE THINGS ON US!
KLNGL

THEY LOOK LIKE... **SHACKLES.**

UNDO THESE! NOW!

HUMPH

THAT MOVE YOU SHOWED US JUST NOW WAS AMAZING...

IT'S HARD TO BELIEVE SOMEONE LIKE YOU IS THE GUARDIAN OF SUCH A SPECIAL POKÉMON MOVE, BUT...

...THAT WAS PRETTY CONVINCING.

WE NEED TO GET STRONGER!
TNK
FSSS
MUCH, MUCH STRONGER!
WILL YOU TEACH US...
...THE SPECIAL MOVES YOU'VE BEEN GUARDING?!
WHY, CER-TAINLY.

KMM
RMM
RMM

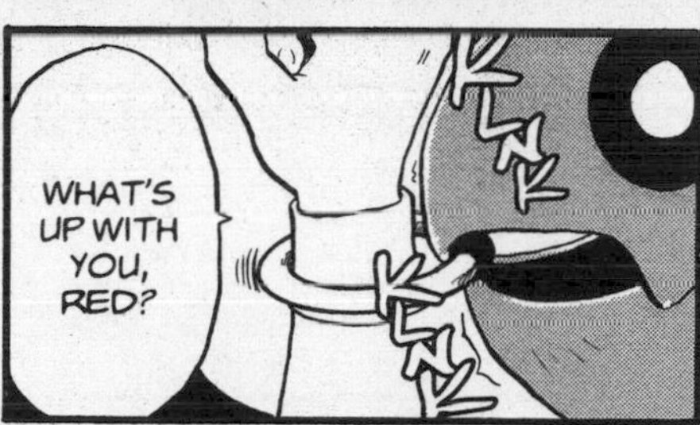
WHAT'S UP WITH YOU, RED?
KLNK
KLNK

THANK YOU FOR CHOOSING OUR SHIP FOR YOUR TRAVEL NEEDS.
NEXT STOP, TWO ISLAND.

HUH? WHAT?
WHAT DO YOU MEAN?
ZZZZZZZ

ARE YOU SERIOUSLY THINKING OF LETTING THAT OLD LADY TRAIN YOU?
SURE I AM!
YOU SAW FOR YOURSELF HOW POWERFUL SHE IS, DIDN'T YOU?

SHE'S CLEARLY MORE POWERFUL THAN US!
AND SHE SAID SHE'S WILLING TO TEACH US THE SPECIAL MOVES SHE'S BEEN GUARDING ALL THIS TIME.
THIS IS A GREAT OPPORTUNITY, RIGHT?

WELL... YOU HAVE A POINT. ..
THAT OLD LADY IS DEFINITELY STRONGER THAN US. AND THAT STORY ABOUT HOW SHE'S THE GUARDIAN OF THE SPECIAL POKÉMON MOVES IS PROBABLY NO LIE.

BUT... ... THAT'S ...

...EXACTLY WHY WE CAN'T TRUST HER!
HUH?!

WHAT IF THAT NOT-SO-INNOCENT-LOOKING OLD LADY TURNS OUT TO BE THE ENEMY?
WHAT IF SHE KNOWS ALL ABOUT THOSE POKÉMON WHO ATTACKED US? AND SHE TURNS OUT TO BE THE MASTERMIND BEHIND IT ALL?

AND WE'RE STUCK WITH HER...
...AND CAN'T GET AWAY!

THE MASTER-MIND...?! YOU REALLY BELIEVE THAT, BLUE?
WELL... IT'S **POSSIBLE**...

CALLING ALL PASSENGERS... THANK YOU FOR SAILING WITH US.

WE ARE NOW ARRIVING AT TWO ISLAND.
YAWN

COME ON! PULL YOURSELF TOGETHER!

STRTCH

BAMP

HEY, THERE'S NO ONE ON THIS ISLAND...
WE'RE THE ONLY ONES WHO GOT OFF THE SHIP HERE TOO!
PHEW!

THIS ISLAND DOESN'T ACCEPT UNSKILLED TRAINERS.
THAT'S RIGHT. AND THAT'S AS IT SHOULD BE.

The Path of Jumping
AND THAT MEANS FIRST YOU MUST BE TESTED!

PHEW! WE'VE FINALLY REACHED YOUR HOUSE...
WHAT ARE YOU TALKING ABOUT? THIS IS JUST THE ENTRANCE.

THE... ENTRANCE?!
CAPE BRINK
MY HOUSE IS LOCATED TWO MILES FROM HERE— AT A PLACE CALLED CAPE BRINK.
THIS IS JUST THE ENTRANCE TO THE LONG, LONG, LONG CORRIDOR THAT LEADS TO MY HOUSE!

GO ON THROUGH!
SQUEEK
SLAM

SO THIS IS WHERE YOU'RE GOING TO TEACH US THOSE SPECIAL MOVES?

SMASH
SILLY CHILD! DID YOU THINK I WOULD REVEAL THEM TO YOU RIGHT AWAY?!

THE FOUNDATION OF ALL MOVES IS STAMINA! ESPECIALLY THE STRENGTH OF YOUR LEGS AND CORE!

HOP TO IT! GET YOUR VENUSAUR AND CHARIZARD OUT!

WE'LL USE VENUSAUR'S VINE AND...
DRAG
DRAG
HERE! HOLD IT, CHARIZARD!

SLIP
BY THE WAY, THE CORRIDOR WILL START TILTING BACKWARDS SOON!

HOP OVER THE VINE LIKE A JUMP ROPE!
AND KEEP JUMPING!

YOU'D BETTER HURRY. I'LL KEEP WATCH FROM OUTSIDE.

JUMP
HFF.
JUMP
HFF.
JUMP
HFF.
JUMP

SO THIS... IS WHAT... THAT SIGN... "THE JUMPING PATH"... MEANS.
JUMP
JUMP
JUMP
HFF.
HFF.
HFF.
HFF.
IF WE FALL OVER, WE GET DRAGGED BACK TO THE BEGINNING AGAIN!
JUMP
JUMP
JUMP
JUMP

UNTIL YOU'VE REACHED THE END OF THE CORRIDOR, OF COURSE!

SO...UM... HOW LONG DO WE HAVE TO DO THIS FOR...?

JUMP
TWENTY-TWO YEARS AGO, A TRAINER WHO TOOK ON THIS CHALLENGE SPENT EIGHT HOURS IN HERE. BUT HE GAVE UP THREE QUARTERS OF THE WAY THROUGH.
JUMP
I HOPE YOU'LL BREAK THAT RECORD AT LEAST.

BY THE WAY, THE TRAINING SESSIONS CHANGE EVERY HALF MILE OR SO.

SAUR, COULD YOU SLOW IT DOWN A LITTLE?!
CHARIZ-ARD, I'M HAVING TROUBLE JUMPING. SPIN IT AROUND FASTER.

HFF.
I HAVE NO IDEA, BUT...

SHE'S A PHONY, RED, JUST LIKE I THOUGHT! HOW ARE WE GOING TO LEARN THOSE SPECIAL MOVES BY DOING THIS?!

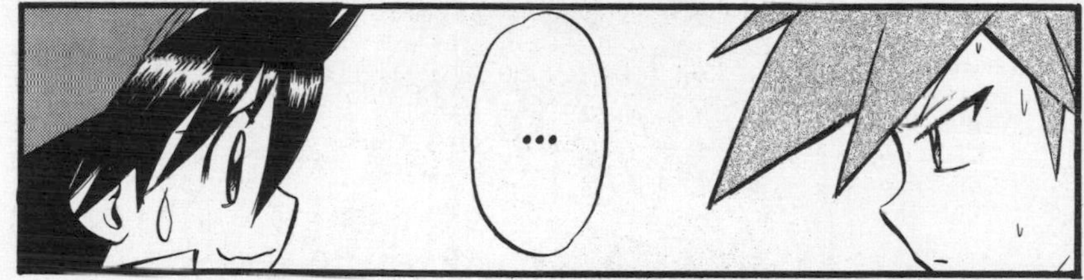
...

WFF
WE DID IT!
JUMP
HFF.
HFF.
JUMP
HFF.
JUMP
HFF.
SAUR, FOLLOW CHARI-ZARD'S LEAD!

The Path of Catching
NOW FOR THE NEXT CORRI-DOR!

WELL, WELL... NOT BAD.
HFF.
HFF.
HFF.

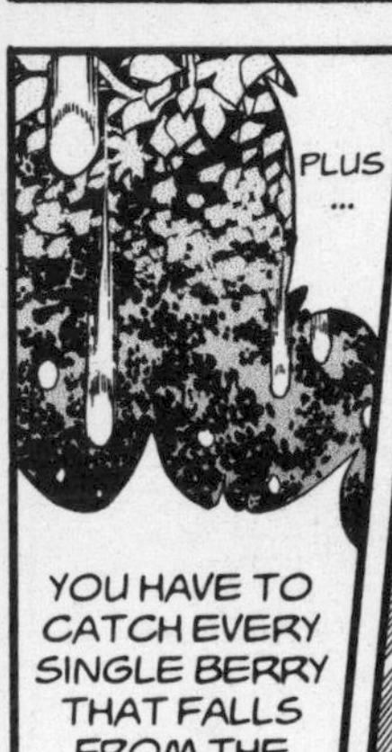
PLUS ...
YOU HAVE TO CATCH EVERY SINGLE BERRY THAT FALLS FROM THE CEILING!

RUN THROUGH THIS MOVING CORRIDOR. BUT IT'S GOING TO MOVE FASTER AS YOU DO!
ZIP

GET ON THE DODRIO I'VE LINED UP FOR YOU!

WSSSSSH

BLUE ...
SNAG
PLONK
OH NO ...!

The Path of Battle
THIS TIME, IT'S THE "PATH OF BATTLE." WHO ARE WE FIGHTING...?
HFF
HFF
HFF

OKAY, THE LAST HALF NOW!
ARE YOU ALL RIGHT, RED?
HFF
HFF

DIDN'T I TELL YOU?

I WILL ONLY TEACH...

...THE SPECIAL MOVE TO **ONE** OF YOU.

POKÉMON ON TEAM RED 2

Snor/Snorlax ♂

Normal

- **LV. 89** (As of Adventure 272)
- **Ability: Immunity**
- **Impish Nature**

Snor is a big eater and is usually sleeping, but in times of trouble, if it's awake, its heavy attacks can be a huge help.

Gyara/Gyarados ♂

Water
Flying

- **LV. 84** (As of Adventure 272)
- **Ability: Intimidate**
- **Lonely Nature**

A Pokémon given to Red by Misty. Gyara is skilled at battles in watery areas and makes good use of many powerful water-type moves.

Aero/Aerodactyl ♂

Rock
Flying

- **LV. 85** (As of Adventure 272)
- **Ability: Rock Head**
- **Hasty Nature**

Aero was revived at Cinnabar Gym from the Old Ember given to Red by Giovanni. This Pokémon comes in handy when Red needs its flying ability.

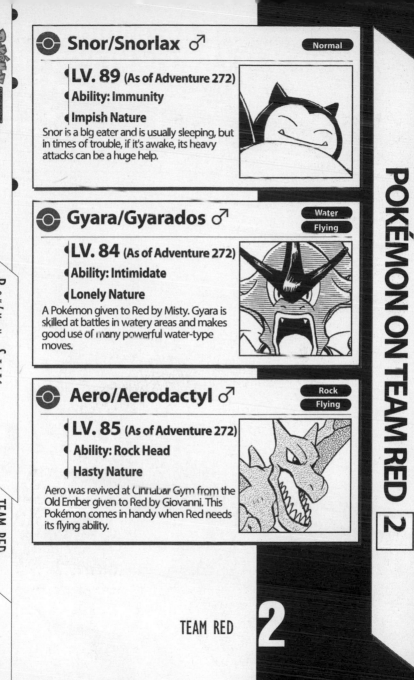

• Adventure 273 •
ed and Blue Make Purple Opponents

I WILL ONLY TEACH...

...THE SPECIAL MOVE TO ONE OF YOU.

!
ZLIP
ZLIP
THIS CORRIDOR MOVES TOO!
ZLIP

JUMP
THE CORRIDOR AT THE PATH OF JUMPING MOVED BACKWARDS!
THE SECOND CORRIDOR AT THE PATH OF CATCHING KEPT MOVING FASTER AND FASTER...
AND NOW IN THE PATH OF BATTLE...
...BOTH SIDES ARE MOVING INDEPENDENTLY!
THAT'S RIGHT! BUT THAT'S NOT ALL...
THE SPEED OF THE CORRIDOR CORRELATES WITH THE ATTACKS OF YOUR POKÉMON.
BAMPF
!
THE CORRIDOR OF THE TRAINER WHO IS ATTACKING WILL MOVE FORWARD FASTER...
WHILE THE CORRIDOR OF THE TRAINER WHO IS RECEIVING DAMAGE WILL SLOW DOWN...
THE TRAINER WHO REACHES THE END OF THE CORRIDOR FIRST WINS!

NOW!
FWSSSH
START YOUR BATTLE!

I NEVER THOUGHT I'D END UP FIGHTING YOU HERE, RED...
YEAH, BLUE... ME NEITHER.
YOU KNOW, IF WE THINK ABOUT IT LOGICALLY...
...THERE'S NO REASON FOR US TO TAKE THIS BATTLE SERIOUSLY.
WHAT DO YOU MEAN?

WELL, ONLY ONE OF US WILL GET TO LEARN THE SPECIAL MOVE IN THE END ANYWAY.
AND I DON'T CARE WHETHER IT'S YOU OR ME.
WE ONLY NEED THAT MOVE TO HELP US FACE THE ENEMY AND HELP GREEN—SO IT DOESN'T MATTER WHO GETS IT.

IF I LOSE ON PURPOSE, THE MOVE WILL BE YOURS...
AND IF **YOU** LOSE ON PURPOSE, THE MOVE WILL BE MINE... IT'S AS SIMPLE AS THAT.
YOU'RE RIGHT...
BUT... ARE YOU REALLY OKAY WITH THAT, BLUE?!

WELL...
Heh...

GOL-DUCK, IRON TAIL!

PORY-GON2, TRI ATTACK!

KRASH

IT WOULD BE EASIER THAT WAY, BUT...

...IF YOU'RE GOING TO BE MY OPPONENT, RED...

...I HAVE TO FIGHT YOU WITH EVERYTHING I'VE GOT!

HEH...

ME TOO!

GYARA! BODY SLAM!
SNOR! STRENGTH!

!
SHNK
WHOOOA!
KLIK

BLUE'S POKÉMON WERE WEAKENED BY YOUR GYARADOS'S ABILITY INTIMIDATE.
BUT THE DAMAGE DEALT BY BLUE'S FIRST ATTACK WAS MORE THAN YOURS... BY THE WAY, EVEN THOUGH THE CORRIDOR IS MOVING, IT'S DEEP ENOUGH TO DIG BELOW IT...

THE MOVEMENT OF THE CORRIDOR IS DIRECTLY CONNECTED TO THE BATTLE, SO...
I GET IT NOW! THAT'S WHAT THAT MEANS!

OKAY! IN THAT CASE ...
... GYARA!

HYPER BEAM!
URGH!
WE'RE SO FAR AWAY, BUT IT'S SUCH A POWERFUL MOVE!
GOLDUCK! HIDE FOR NOW!
DIG DIG DIG
DIG!
I'LL HAVE THE ADVANTAGE WITH MY NEXT ATTACK BECAUSE GOLDUCK WILL HAVE THE BENEFIT OF SURPRISE!
...!

RMBL
RMBL
SNOR!
EARTH-QUAKE!
RMBL
RMBL
AH, NUTS!
...IT'LL RECEIVE **TWICE** AS MUCH DAMAGE!
EARTH-QUAKE IS A MOVE THAT AFFECTS THE WHOLE AREA...
IT WILL INFLICT DAMAGE ON BOTH GOLDUCK AND PORYGON2.
THAT'S NOT ALL! GOLDUCK IS USING DIG, SO...

IT'S PARALYZED! THE TRI ATTACK IT RECEIVED AT THE BEGINNING MUST HAVE TAKEN EFFECT!

OH NO!

TINGLE TINGLE

GYARA ?!

WELL DONE, SNOR, GYARA!

THIS SURE BRINGS BACK MEMORIES, RED...
...OF THAT TIME BACK IN THE POKÉMON LEAGUE WHEN WE FOUGHT EACH OTHER ...
WHAT A THRILL!

• Adventure 274 •
Double Dealing with Deoxys

WHZZZZ
KLCK
GRAB

SEIS-
MIC
TOSS!
KA
THUD

THOSE FOUR ARMS GOT THE BETTER OF ME AGAIN!
AND THE SPEED OF SCIZOR DIVING DOWN TO THE FLOOR ADDED TO THE POWER OF THE TOSS!
MACHAMP! GO FOR THE FINISH!
SWISH
FWIP

LOW
KICK!

HM ...
...SO IT'S THE PERFECT MOVE TO ATTACK SNOR WITH!
LOW KICK DOES MORE DAMAGE TO HEAVIER POKÉMON ...
SNOR!

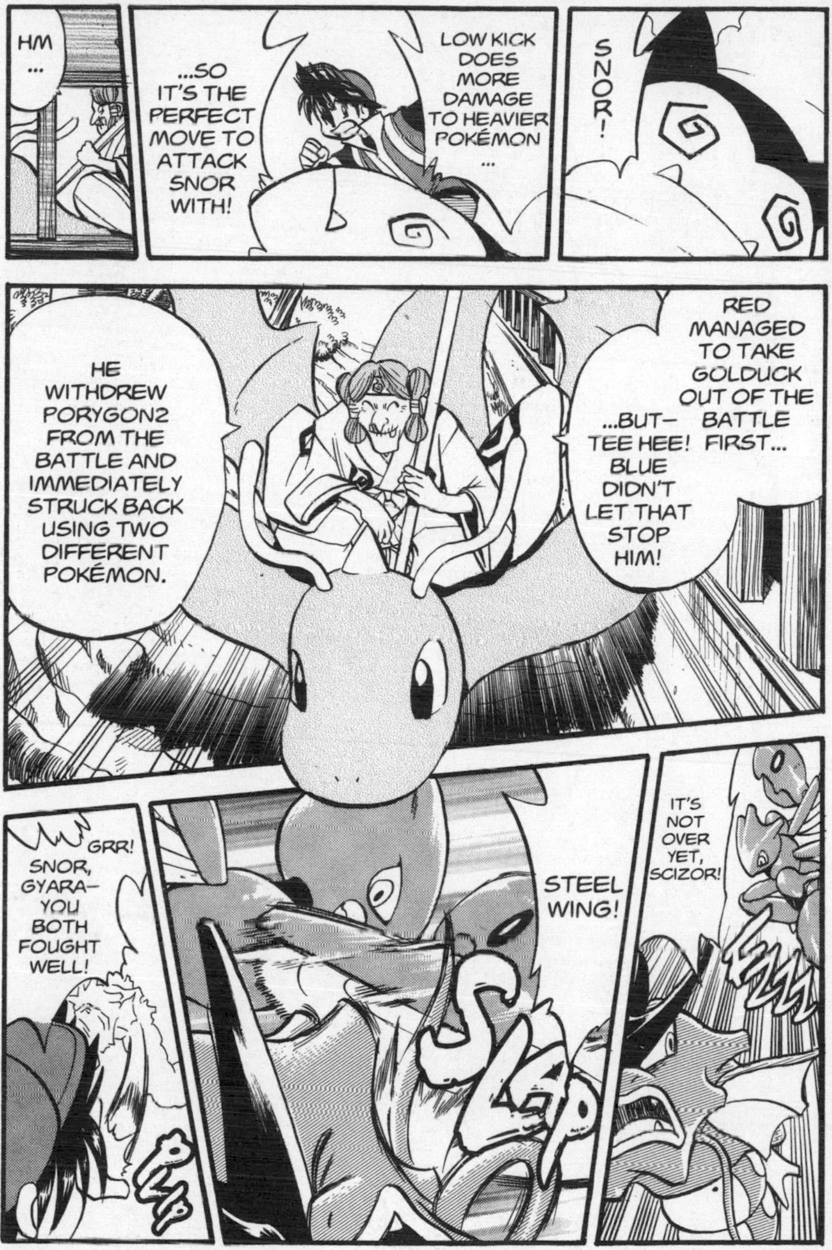

RED MANAGED TO TAKE GOLDUCK OUT OF THE BATTLE FIRST...
...BUT— TEE HEE! BLUE DIDN'T LET THAT STOP HIM!
HE WITHDREW PORYGON2 FROM THE BATTLE AND IMMEDIATELY STRUCK BACK USING TWO DIFFERENT POKÉMON.
IT'S NOT OVER YET, SCIZOR!
FZZZ
STEEL WING!
SLAP
GRR! SNOR, GYARA-YOU BOTH FOUGHT WELL!
PUMP

BOOM
AERO! PIKA!
SMAK
AERO'S ABILITY IS ROCK HEAD!
IT WON'T RECEIVE ANY RECOIL DAMAGE, NO MATTER HOW MANY TIMES IT USES TAKE DOWN! IT CAN JUST KEEP ON ATTACKING!
TNK
TNK
TNK
IT'LL BE AN AERIAL BATTLE! GO!

CR
BLUE HAS CAUGHT UP WITH HIM! WHAT NOW?
DRAGON CLAW!
USH
COME BACK, SCIZOR!
ZLOOP
THIS IS OUR CHANCE, PIKA!
KRCKL
KR
CKL
!
BEND

ZZZOP ZZZOP

RHYDON!

THE GOAL IS RIGHT IN FRONT OF US!
AND I'M GOING TO WIN!
NO! IT'S NOT OVER YET!
I'LL FIGHT TILL THE BITTER END...!
PIKA!
BOING
IF I CAN'T ATTACK YOU WITH PIKA'S LIGHTNING...
KICK
...THEN I'LL JUST HAVE TO ATTACK YOU DIRECTLY!
TING
TING
IRON TAIL!

SMASH
SMASH
ZIP
TCH!
STEP

HFF.
HFF.
GASP.
HFF.
HFF.
GASP.
GASP.

WHICH OF US... MADE IT... FIRST? YOU...OR ME?
HFF.
HFF.
HFF.
DUNNO... IT LOOKED LIKE...WE BOTH GOT HERE...AT THE SAME TIME.

HEY, GRANDMA!
WHICH OF US WON?!

MMM

SQUEAK
GRAND-MA...?!

?!

AHH
THAT SHADOW ...!

IT'S THE SAME AS...!

WISH

THIS IS NO TIME TO COMPLAIN! WE HAVE TO DO SOME-THING OR IT'LL GET US TOO!
WHY DOES IT HAVE TO ATTACK US WHEN WE'RE DEAD TIRED ...?
NO!
ARGH!
YOINK
SHING
THERE'S SOME KIND OF... ENGRAV-ING ON MINE!
THE BRACELETS THAT OLD LADY ATTACHED TO OUR WRISTS ARE **SHINING...**
BLAST... BURN...
FRENZY PLANT...

ROAAAARR

FRENZY PLANT!

BLAST BURN!

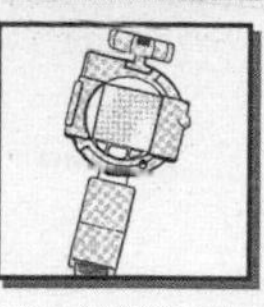

BLUE

BLUE IS RED'S RIVAL AND BEST FRIEND, AS WELL AS THE RUNNER UP OF THE NINTH POKÉMON LEAGUE AND A SKILLED TRAINER. THE GREAT POKÉMON RESEARCHER PROFESSOR OAK IS BLUE'S GRAND-FATHER, AND DAISY OAK IS HIS OLDER SISTER. BLUE IS USUALLY CALM AND COMPOSED, AND IS EXCEPTIONALLY GOOD AT FIGURING OUT HIS OPPONENT'S STRATEGY IN BATTLE. HE IS CURRENTLY INVESTIGATING THE MYSTERY AT THE SEVII ISLANDS WITH RED.

- **Birthplace: Pallet Town**
- **Birthday: November 22**
- **Blood Type: AB**
- **Age: 16 Years Old**
  (As of the Fifth Chapter)
- **Prizes Won: Gym Leader Tryouts. Currently the Gym Leader of Viridian Gym.**

• Adventure 275 •
A Vicious Cycle of Possibilities

Pokémon Adventures FireRed & LeafGreen

The Fifth Chapter

MEANWHILE, AS RED AND BLUE ARE TRAINING WITH ULTIMA...

VROOM VROOM

HEH HEH HEH! SO **THIS** IS THREE ISLAND!

LOOKS LIKE A GREAT PLACE TO **TEAR APART**!

IT'S ALSO KNOWN AS KIN ISLAND.
KIN ISLAND? HOW COME?
BECAUSE THIS ISLAND LOOKS LIKE THE PARENT AND THAT SMALL ISLAND CONNECTED BY BOND BRIDGE LOOKS LIKE ITS CHILD!
THERE'S A FOREST SOME-WHERE 'ROUND HERE CALLED BERRY FOREST ...

COME BACK HERE ...!

VRMM

GOTCHA!

AIIEE!

SKREECH

WAHHH! I'M SORRY!
SWISH
SHUT UP! QUITCHER CRYING!
YOU'RE IN OUR WAY!
SHWIPP

HUH
?

THEY WENT OFF WITH THAT OLD LADY...
...AND I HAVEN'T THE FOGGI-EST HOW THEY'RE HOLDIN' UP.
PHEW ...
I SURE HOPE RED AND BLUE ARE ALL RIGHT...
ONE ISLAND...
POKÉMON NETWORK CENTER...

OH!
I'VE GOTTA TAKE ALL THIS EQUIPMENT DOWN AND FIX THE POKÉMON TRANSPORTER.
BUT I DON'T HAVE TIME TO BOTHER 'BOUT THEM.

GREEN ...

SHE... SHE STILL HASN'T COME TO...

WE NEED TO GO.
TAKE CARE OF GREEN FOR US, WOULD YOU PLEASE, BILL...?

OF COURSE. I'LL KEEP AN EYE ON HER, F'SURE.
THANK YOU.

HEY! HOLD ON A SEC, RED!
THERE'S SOME-THIN' I'VE BEEN MEANIN' TO ASK YA!

ON THE *SEAGALLOP*, YA TOLD ME...

...YA CAME HERE 'CAUSE PROFESSOR OAK ASKED YA TO.

THAT'S RIGHT. WE FOUND A FAME CHECKER WITH A RECORDING OF PROFESSOR OAK ON IT...AND AN ENVELOPE WITH A TRI-PASS FOR THE *SEAGALLOP* INSIDE.

THERE WERE THREE SETS OF 'EM, RIGHT?
FOR RED, BLUE AND GREEN.
NOD
THAT DOESN'T MAKE ANY SENSE, DOES IT?

GREEN HAD HER TRI-PASS WITH HER.

SEEMS LIKE SHE MET UP WITH PROFES-SOR OAK BEFORE Y'ALL.

SO WHAT D'YOU FIGGER WAS INSIDE THE ENVELOPE ADDRESSED TO GREEN ...?!
AND WHAT KIND OF MESSAGE WAS RECORDED ON **HER** FAME CHECKER?
...

TO TELL YOU THE TRUTH, I WAS WON-DERING THE SAME THING.

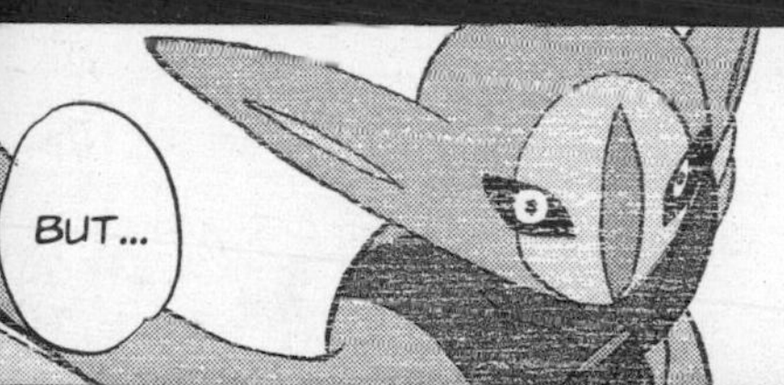
WELL, THE ANSWER IS INSIDE GREEN'S ENVELOPE AND FAME CHECKER...
BUT...

IT'S ADDRESSED TO HER FROM PROFESSOR OAK...
SHE SHOULD BE THE ONE TO OPEN IT.

TO GREEN
SO I LEFT IT NEXT TO GREEN'S BED.

RIGHT! SORRY, GOTTA RUN!
I'M READY! COME DOWN TO THE NETWORK MACHINE QUICK!

YOU'RE RIGHT. WHAT THE HECK IS GOIN' ON? ARGH! I CAN'T MAKE ANY SENSE OF IT!
Think, think...

THE WHOLE SYSTEM SEEMS TO HAVE BEEN TAKEN OVER BY SOME SORT OF POWERFUL EXTERNAL FORCE...

URRRGH...

STOP!
HELP ME...

TOSS

SNIFF! URK...

FOOSH
HFF.
HFF.
HFF.

KRNCH

HEY! **HEY**! YOU G-G-GOTTA HELP ME!

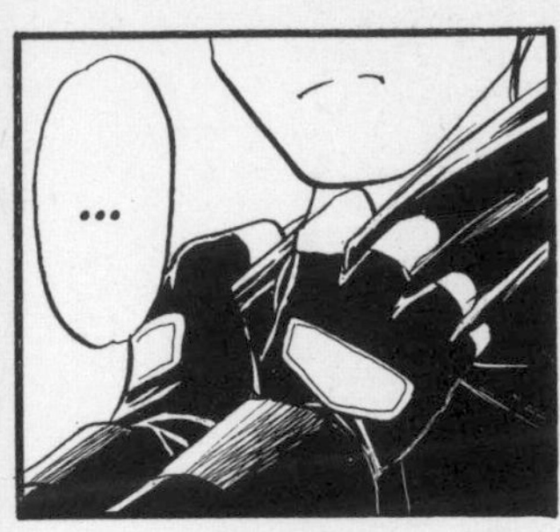

SMAK
NNGH!
WHAT'D YOU DO THAT FOR?!
WHOSE SIDE ARE YOU ON, ANYWAY?!
BOOM
BOOM
BOOM

ROCK TOMB!
PATHETIC.
YOU CLAIM TO BE EVIL— SO WHY NOT GO ALL THE WAY WITH IT?
THERE IS NOTHING SO DIS-GRACEFUL AS DOING SOME-THING HALF-BAKED!
ALSO ...

AND ITS NAME IS... **DEOXYS**!

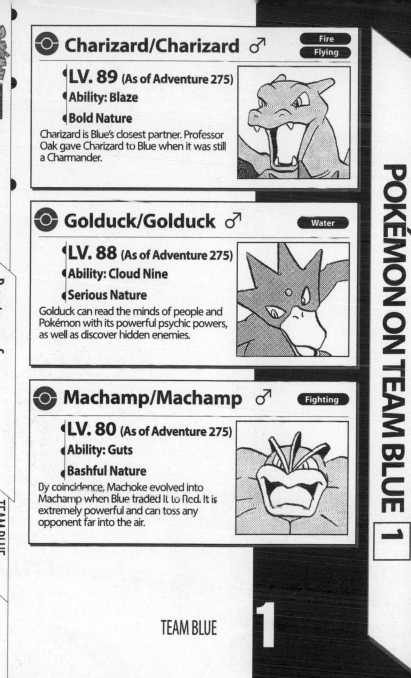

Charizard/Charizard 

Fire
Flying

- **LV. 89 (As of Adventure 275)**
- **Ability: Blaze**
- **Bold Nature**

Charizard is Blue's closest partner. Professor Oak gave Charizard to Blue when it was still a Charmander.

Golduck/Golduck 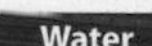

Water

- **LV. 88 (As of Adventure 275)**
- **Ability: Cloud Nine**
- **Serious Nature**

Golduck can read the minds of people and Pokémon with its powerful psychic powers, as well as discover hidden enemies.

Machamp/Machamp 

Fighting

- **LV. 80 (As of Adventure 275)**
- **Ability: Guts**
- **Bashful Nature**

By coincidence, Machoke evolved into Machamp when Blue traded it to Red. It is extremely powerful and can toss any opponent far into the air.

TEAM BLUE

POKéMON ADVENTURES
FIRERED & LEAFGREEN
The Fifth Chapter

FRENZY PLANT!
BLAST BURN!
WE DID IT!
SO THIS IS THE SPECIAL MOVE THAT OLD LADY WAS TALKING ABOUT!
STGGR
ZLIP

KRCKL
KRASH
!

TMP
HMPH! IT COULD TELL WHERE WE WERE GOING TO ATTACK SO IT DODGED!
LET'S ATTACK IT AGAIN!
TMP

!
THEY CAN'T MOVE BECAUSE OF THE IMPACT OF THE BACKLASH OF OUR ATTACK...
DOES THAT MEAN WE CAN'T USE THAT MOVE TWICE IN A ROW?
RED ...
IT DIDN'T ACTUALLY DODGE OUR ATTACK... WE MISSED.

STEP
WE USED OUR NEW MOVE WITHOUT ANY KNOWLEDGE OF ITS POWER, ACCURACY, OR THE IMPACT IT WOULD HAVE ON OUR OWN POKÉMON...
WE DIDN'T STRAT-EGIZE WELL.

!
STEP
WE DON'T KNOW HOW TO HANDLE THAT MOVE.

NOT EXACTLY ...

!
WHAT ARE YOU UP TO NOW, GRANDMA?!
ARE YOU TRYING TO TRICK US AND LIE TO US?!
TRICK YOU...? LIE TO YOU...? HOW RUDE!
I'VE TOLD YOU NO FALSEHOODS!
YOU EXPECT US TO BELIEVE THAT?!

LOOK! THE ENEMY THAT ATTACKED US IS WITH YOU!

SO YOU **ARE** THE MASTER-MIND BEHIND THIS INCIDENT AFTER ALL!

!

WOM

WOM

WOM

DITTO ?!

ARE YOU... GREEN'S DITTO?!

IT FOLLOWED YOU FROM ONE ISLAND, RED, BY CLINGING TO THE TOP OF YOUR BACKPACK.

WE BECAME FRIENDS WHILE YOU WERE TRAINING.

WE WERE ONLY PLAYING TOGETHER. YOU MISTOOK OUR GAME FOR AN ATTACK ON ME.

...

AND BY THE WAY...
I WASN'T LYING WHEN I SAID I WOULD ONLY TEACH MY SPECIAL MOVE TO ONE OF YOU.

BUT YOU TWO HAVE EXACTLY THE SAME STRENGTH AND YOU WERE TIED AT THE FINISH LINE...

...SO I DECIDED TO TEACH THE MOVE TO BOTH OF YOU AFTER ALL.

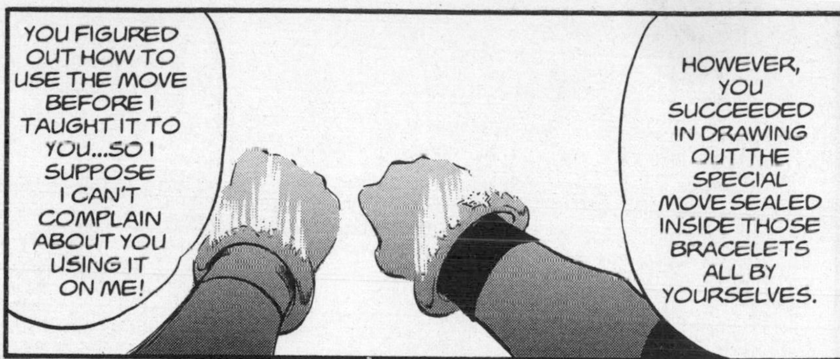
HOWEVER, YOU SUCCEEDED IN DRAWING OUT THE SPECIAL MOVE SEALED INSIDE THOSE BRACELETS ALL BY YOURSELVES.
YOU FIGURED OUT HOW TO USE THE MOVE BEFORE I TAUGHT IT TO YOU...SO I SUPPOSE I CAN'T COMPLAIN ABOUT YOU USING IT ON ME!

SNAP

IT'S UP TO YOU TO PRACTICE UNTIL YOU CAN HIT YOUR TARGET PROPERLY.

ULTIMA, WE OWE YOU AN—

AND ONE MORE THING!

I DON'T KNOW WHAT'S GOING ON, BUT THAT DITTO SEEMED PRETTY DESPERATE.
IT USED TRANSFORM TO SHOW ME WHAT HAPPENED ON THE *SEAGALLOP*.
THIS ENEMY OF YOURS MUST BE **VERY POWERFUL.**
IF YOU'RE GOING TO FACE IT WITH THE SPECIAL MOVE I'VE BEEN GUARDING ALL THIS TIME...
...WELL, THAT WOULD MAKE ME PROUD! HEH HEH...
...
GOOD LUCK!
OH...

BOW
THANK YOU VERY MUCH!
WE GRATEFULLY ACCEPT YOUR SPECIAL MOVE!

DITTO, YOU FOLLOWED US ALL THE WAY HERE...
YOU MUST WANT TO HELP GREEN TOO.

THERE'S SOME-THING I WANT TO ASK YOU THAT MIGHT HELP US HELP HER...
LIFT

I WANT YOU TO USE TRANSFORM AGAIN, OKAY?
WHAT ARE YOU UP TO, BLUE...?

RED, DIDN'T IT SEEM KIND OF WEIRD TO YOU...?
WOM
WOM
WHAT?

THE ENEMY'S **SHAPE.**

THINK ABOUT IT... WE LEARNED WHAT THE ENEMY LOOKED LIKE FROM THE IMAGE RECORDED ON GREEN'S SILPH SCOPE.
!

BUT SOME-THING DOESN'T MAKE SENSE...
THE IMAGE WE SAW... AND THE SHAPE DITTO TRANS-FORMED INTO...

THEY'RE SIMILAR, BUT... THERE ARE A BUNCH OF DIFFERENCES.
COME TO THINK OF IT... YOU'RE RIGHT!
BUT WHAT DOES IT MEAN...?
IS THERE MORE THAN ONE ENEMY? OR DID IT EVOLVE?
OR... MAYBE THIS POKÉMON CHANGES FORMES DEPENDING ON THE SITUATION AND BATTLE-STYLE...
GULP
THIS INFORMATION COULD MEAN THE DIFFERENCE BETWEEN VICTORY AND DEFEAT!
WOM
WOM
IF WE CAN'T FIND THE ANSWER TO THIS QUESTION, WE'LL PROBABLY...
...LOSE.

I WANT YA TO USE 'EM TO...

...TRAVEL TO FOUR ISLAND RIGHT AWAY.

Rainbow Pass

IT'S AP-PEARED HERE NOW!
WHAT DO YA THINK?!

WAIT... WHAT'S SO IMPOR-TANT THAT YOU HAVE TO TALK TO US ABOUT IT RIGHT AWAY?!
IT'S URGENT!
SHAKE A LEG!

THE ENEMY THAT ATTACKED Y'ALL, BLUE, AND GREEN!

IT'S COME TA THREE ISLAND!

I'VE SENT TWO OF 'EM TO THE POKÉMON CENTER ON TWO ISLAND. COME DOWN HEAH AS SOON AS YOU PICK 'EM UP!

YOU CAN'T GET TA FOUR ISLAND AND BEYOND WITH THE TRI-PASS YOU'VE GOT. YOU NEED THE RAINBOW PASS FER THAT.

I'LL BE WAITIN' FOR YOU AT ICEFALL CAVE ON FOUR ISLAND.

WHOA! IT'S COLD HERE!
THIS IS THE CAVE BILL WAS TALKING ABOUT, RIGHT?
THE TEMPERATURE DOESN'T FLUCTUATE MUCH UNDER-GROUND, BUT STILL... IT'S MUCH WARMER OUTSIDE ON ONE ISLAND AND TWO ISLAND.

YOU'RE RIGHT ...
THE ICE-TYPE POKÉMON WHO LIVE DOWN HERE MUST LOWER THE TEMPERA-TURE.

HUH ?
TING

TING

!
WZNNNNN

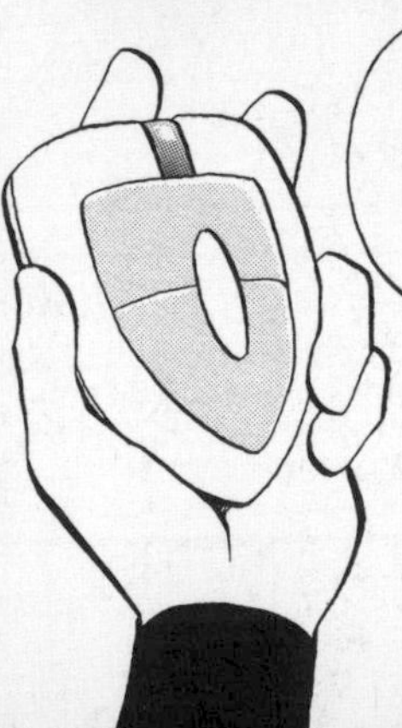
WHAT'S THIS?

LUNGE
GRR
IS THAT EXEGGUTOR ATTACKING US?!
GREAT!
CHARIZARD!
THIS IS A PERFECT OPPORTUNITY FOR US TO PRACTICE!
BOM
RMBL
BLAST BURN!
WHOA! HOLD IT, HOLD IT, HOLD IT!
JUMP

BILL!

WHAT WAS THAT ALL ABOUT ?!
SORRY, SORRY! I JUST WANTED TO TEST THAT GADGET OUT!

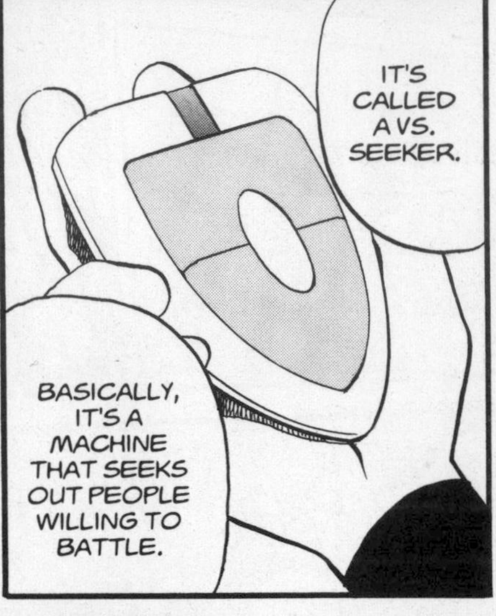
IT'S CALLED A VS. SEEKER.
BASICALLY, IT'S A MACHINE THAT SEEKS OUT PEOPLE WILLING TO BATTLE.

IT'S PRETTY USEFUL. IT FINDS TRAINERS READY TO FIGHT WITHIN A CERTAIN RADIUS AND SHINES A LIGHT IN THEIR DIRECTION!
I GOT IT FOR Y'ALL. THOUGHT IT MIGHT COME IN HANDY.
IT SEEKS PEOPLE WHO ARE READY TO FIGHT, HUH...?
!

THAT MEANS...THIS DEVICE WILL TELL US WHEN THE ENEMY IS APPROACHING TO ATTACK US, RIGHT?!
NAH.
IT ONLY SEARCHES FER TRAINERS WILLIN' TO CHALLENGE YA TO A BATTLE FAIR AND SQUARE.
FWUMP

THEN IT ISN'T ANY USE TO US. NOW HURRY UP AND TELL US ABOUT THE ENEMY!
TOSS

I THOUGHT YOU'D ASK THAT...
BUT YOU'LL FIGURE IT OUT ON YOUR OWN RIGHT QUICK.

I'LL CUT TO THE CHASE!

GULP

A LITTLE LOCAL GIRL NAMED LOSTELLE...

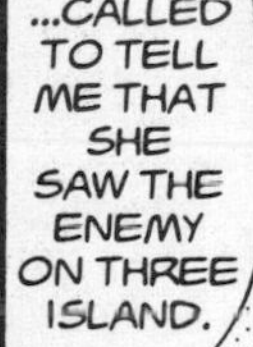
...CALLED TO TELL ME THAT SHE SAW THE ENEMY ON THREE ISLAND.

LOSTELLE WAS BEING PICKED ON BY A BUNCH OF BIKERS WHO WERE TEARIN' UP THE ISLAND...

...BUT SOMETHIN' APPEARED OUT OF THE BLUE AND BEAT 'EM ALL UP.

AND THAT SOME-THIN' HAP-PENED TO BE... THE ENEMY!

WHAT?!
IT HELPED A LITTLE GIRL?!

WELL, I DON'T KNOW IF IT WAS HELPIN' HER OR JUST WANTED TA PICK A FIGHT.
BUT THE POINT OF THIS STORY COMES AFTER THAT!

HERE'S ...
RSTL

UM... HE LOOKED ABOUT THE SAME AGE AS MY DAD. I DREW A PICTURE OF HIM. I'LL FAX IT TO YOU...

ACCORDING TO LOSTELLE, THE ENEMY TOOK OFF AND THEN... A MAN SHOWED UP.

...THE FAX!
TA DA

!

THE MARK ON THE CHEST!
AND ...
...THOSE CLOTHES ...

IT'S GIOVANNI!

I THOUGHT TEAM ROCKET WAS DISBANDED... AND TO TOP IT OFF, THIS IS THEIR **BOSS**!

I COULDN'T BELIEVE MAH EYES EITHER!

GIOVANNI...
WE'LL HAVE TO FACE HIM—AND FIGHT HIM—AGAIN!

I DON'T KNOW IF YOUR ENEMY IS GIOVANNI'S POKÉMON...
...OR JUST A WILD POKÉMON HE WAS GOIN' AFTER TO CAPTURE.
THE CONNECTION BETWEEN 'EM IS STILL A DOWNRIGHT MYSTERY.

BUT AS LONG AS TEAM ROCKET'S INVOLVED...
RIGHT...

PERFECT. WE CAN FIND OUT MORE ABOUT THE ENEMY BY FINDING TEAM ROCKET THEN.
SEE? NOW DO YA UNNERSTAND WHY YOU NEED THE VS. SEEKER?

I HAD YA MEET ME AT ICEFALL CAVE...
...'CAUSE THERE'S A RUMOR GOIN' 'ROUND THAT SOME PEOPLE WHO'RE THE SPITTIN' IMAGE OF TEAM ROCKET HAVE BEEN GOIN' IN AND OUT OF THIS CAVE.

TNG

UP TILL NOW, ALL WE COULD DO WAS WAIT FOR SOMETHING TO HAPPEN... BUT NOW WE HAVE SOME-BODY TO GO AFTER!
SNAP
LET'S FIND PEOPLE WILLING TO FIGHT US!

SHNG
THAT WAY!

FWIP
!
WIP

LUNGE

IT DOESN'T WANT US TO GO ANY DEEPER INTO THE CAVE.
THEY'VE CLEARLY RECEIVED ORDERS FROM SOME TRAINER.

TEAM ROCKET MUST BE IN HERE SOME-WHERE.
OKAY, SAUR ...

!
FWOO OSH

KRIK
KRIK
KRIK
KRIK

I'M JUST AS MAD AT THEM AS YOU ARE...

...FOR TEARING UP MY HOMETOWN!

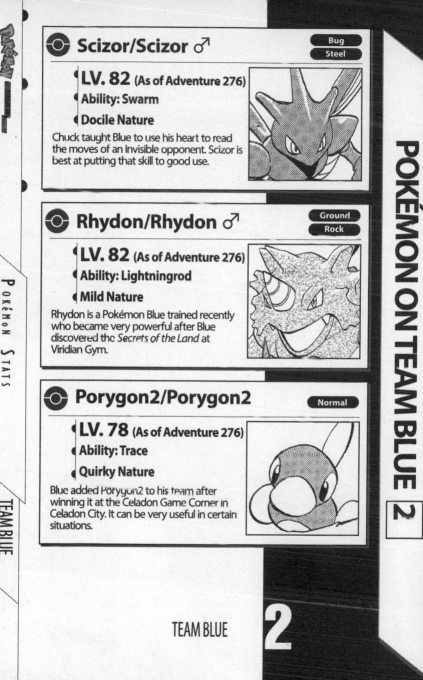

Scizor/Scizor ♂

Bug
Steel

LV. 82 (As of Adventure 276)

Ability: Swarm

Docile Nature

Chuck taught Blue to use his heart to read the moves of an invisible opponent. Scizor is best at putting that skill to good use.

Rhydon/Rhydon ♂

Ground
Rock

LV. 82 (As of Adventure 276)

Ability: Lightningrod

Mild Nature

Rhydon is a Pokémon Blue trained recently who became very powerful after Blue discovered the *Secrets of the Land* at Viridian Gym.

Porygon2/Porygon2

Normal

LV. 78 (As of Adventure 276)

Ability: Trace

Quirky Nature

Blue added Porygon2 to his team after winning it at the Celadon Game Corner in Celadon City. It can be very useful in certain situations.

• Adventure 277 •
A Beastly Cold Reception

YOU'RE ...
...ONE OF THE KANTO ELITE FOUR!

KLANG
SNAP
SO I'M BACK!
I NEVER EXPECTED TO SEE YOU HERE, THOUGH.
CLOY-STER, SPIKE CANNON!
FOOF FOOF FOOF FOOF

ZOOPAH
IT DOESN'T REALLY MATTER WHO I'M FIGHTING, BUT I AM CURIOUS ABOUT ONE THING...
SHE'S STRONG ...!
CHONK
IS TEAM ROCKET REALLY INSIDE ICEFALL CAVE?
SMASH
I OVER-HEARD YOU TALKING ABOUT IT...
ARE YOU CER-TAIN?
...
HEH... YOU DON'T WANT TO DISCUSS THIS WITH ME, DO YOU?
THAT'S UNDER-STAND-ABLE.
I'LL JUST CHECK FOR MYSELF IF TEAM ROCKET WAS BEHIND THIS ATTACK...
RMBL
RMBL
?!
RMBL
NO NEED. THE KIDS GOT IT RIGHT.
!

CRASH
AAH!
SMASH
WHERE ARE YOU?!
BOOM
KRNCH
WE'RE THE ONES WHO ORDERED THOSE POKÉMON TO ATTACK YOU...
AND WE ARE...TEAM ROCKET!

KLANG
SH
URGH...
ARGH!
SIGH... THESE POKÉMON WERE SO WEAK I CAPTURED THEM EASILY. THEY'RE BASICALLY USELESS.
KICK
THIS IS WHAT YOU GET FOR...
...WASTING MY TIME AND ENERGY!
KWASMAK
I ONLY USE POKÉMON WHO ARE USEFUL.
AIN'T THAT RIGHT, FORRETRESS?

WE'VE CAPTURED RED AND BLUE OF PALLET TOWN.

BUT THINGS ARE GOING AS PLANNED.

RED!

BLUE!

TWIST

FRENZY PLANT!

BLAST BURN!

SLAM

OOPS.

THAT'S ENOUGH PLAYING AROUND, CARR.

HA HA HA! AMAZING! THOSE ARE SOME POWERFUL MOVES!

BUT THEY'RE USELESS IF YOU CAN'T HIT ME WITH THEM!

HURRY UP AND GET THE JOB DONE!

ALL RIGHT, SIRD.

ALLOW ME TO INTRODUCE MYSELF AND MY COMPAN-IONS.
WE ARE THE THREE BEASTS— THE SPECIAL FORCES OF TEAM ROCKET AND OUR BOSS'S MOST LOYAL SOLDIERS.
SIRD!
CARR!
AND I'M ORM.

BOSS?! YOU'RE REFERRING TO—
—GIOVANNI, OF COURSE.
WHAT ARE YOU PLANNING TO DO?!
WHAT NEFARIOUS SCHEME IS GIOVANNI TRYING TO ACCOMPLISH NOW WITH THAT MYSTERY POKÉMON?!
AND WHY WERE WE—AND GREEN AND HER PARENTS—ATTACKED?!
TELL US!
NO WAY.
JUMP
GRRRR!
RED! YOU CAN'T JUST CHARGE STRAIGHT AT THEM LIKE THAT!
ZIP

P.F
FAM
BOOM
RM BL RM BL
SIGH... IT'S OVER.
IT'S A BIT DISAPPOINTING TO SEE THEM GO THAT QUICKLY...

NO... WAIT!

JUST BEFORE THE EXPLOSION...
...THAT WOMAN USED SLOWKING'S DIG TO ESCAPE!

WHAT DID I TELL YOU, CARR!
IT'S OKAY, SIRD!
WE'LL JUST HAVE TO...
...FORCE THEM OUT OF THEIR HIDING PLACES!

HFF
HFF
HFF
HFF
HFF
HFF
HFF

WHY IS THIS ROOM FILLED WITH POKÉMON PLUSH TOYS?
IT'S MY HOUSE! YOU GOT A PROBLEM WITH MY INTERIOR DECORATION?!

CITIZENS OF THE SEVII ISLANDS, IF YOU WISH US TO HALT OUR ATTACK, HAND OVER RED, BLUE AND GREEN OF PALLET TOWN!

WANTED

TEAM ROCKET IS ABOUT TO LAUNCH AN ALL-OUT ATTACK ON YOUR LAND!

• Adventure 278 •
Put Your Beast Foot Forward

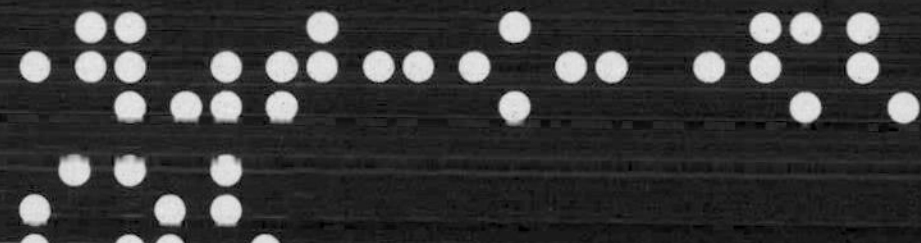

POKÉMON ADVENTURES
FIRERED & LEAFGREEN
The Fifth Chapter

RMBL RMBL

HUH? THE ISLAND IS SHAK-ING!

IT FEELS LIKE ALL OF FOUR ISLAND IS VIBRATING ...

RMBL

!

RSTL

WHAT'S GOING ON?!

FOR STARTERS...
...I'M GOING TO ATTACK FIVE ISLAND.

ORM WILL ATTACK SIX ISLAND.

AND SIRD WILL VISIT SEVEN ISLAND—AND DEMOLISH IT. YOU HAVE BEEN WARNED.

WHOEVER IS PROTECTING RED, BLUE AND GREEN OF PALLET TOWN...
IF YOU WISH US TO CANCEL OUR ATTACK...

...HAND THOSE KIDS OVER TO US IMMEDI- ATELY!
BL RM BL
RM
BL RM

AN ALL-OUT ATTACK ON THE SEVII ISLANDS ...?!

...

BUT WHY IN TARNATION DO THEY WANNA...

... CAPTURE RED, BLUE AND GREEN?

WHAT'S IN IT FOR THEM?!

I HAVEN'T THE FOGGIEST ...

THAT'S JUST TH' KIND OF ROTTEN BLACKMAIL TEAM ROCKET WOULD ENGAGE IN!

BUT NOW THAT WE KNOW THEY'RE AFTER US, WE CAN'T HOLE UP HERE ANY LONGER.

IF THEY WANT ME, I'LL GIVE THEM WHAT THEY WANT!

I'M GOING TOO.

HOLD IT, BLUE!

FWUMP

...THAT MEANS I SHOULD GO TO SEVEN ISLAND!

IS THAT OKAY WITH YOU GUYS?

LORELEI ...

YEAH, THANKS!

RMBL RMBL
SHDDR!
DID YOU SAY SOMETHING?
GLARE
ALL RIGHT, ALL RIGHT. I'LL TAKE YOU. AHAHAHA...
TCH... YOU THINK THE SEAGALLOP IS SOME KIND OF TAXI OR SOMETHING?
I haven't had a moment's rest!
MUMBL MUMBL
LEAD THE WAY.
Oh joy.
THERE IT IS, RED! FIVE ISLAND!
YAY!
I'M GOING ON AHEAD OF YOU GUYS!
WU
FLAP FLAP

WELL THEN...
TIME TO LAUNCH OUR ATTACK.
I'LL PROBABLY BLOW THE WHOLE ISLAND OUT OF THE WATER!
AND MY ATTACKS ARE AWESOME!
WOOOPF
BOOOM
HA HA HA HA HA!
KWA
DRAGONBREATH!
FOOOM

RMBL
I'LL DESTROY EVERYTHING.
RESORT GORGEOUS AND THE MEMORIAL PILLAR TOO...

YOU WANNA ATTACK HEAD-ON, FORRETRESS?!
HMM... I'M GETTING BORED OF BATTLING FROM UP HERE.

OKAY THEN! FLY STRAIGHT INTO THE POKÉMON CENTER AND...
SMASH
TIING
EXPLOSION!
KABOOOOOM!

WHAT'S UP WITH YOU, FORRE-TRESS?
YOU DIDN'T EXPLODE? YOU'RE JUST SMOLDER-ING?
FSS
SSS
HUH?
EXPLOSION AGAIN...?
I'M NOT FALLING FOR THAT ANYMORE!

YOU HAVE SOME NERVE CHASING AFTER ME!
I DON'T KNOW HOW YOU STOPPED MY FORRETRESS FROM USING EXPLOSION, BUT...
...I DO NOT APPRECIATE YOUR MEDDLING!
HOW DARE YOU STAND IN MY WAY?
I'LL DESTROY YOU! THAT'LL STOP YOU FROM TRYING YOUR LITTLE TRICKS ON ME!
MUNCH
HAHA-HAHA! SERVES YOU RIGHT!
!
SHAKE
SHAKE

!
MMMPH
MY BRAVE FRIEND POLI PREVENTED YOUR FORRETRESS FROM USING EXPLOSION.
POLI'S ABILITY IS DAMP, WHICH PREVENTS EXPLOSION MOVES!
PLUS ...
...POLI IS A RELIABLE CLOSE-COMBAT FIGHTER!
STOP THIS ...
... FOCUS PUNCH!

TINK
TINK
TINK
THIS IS UNFORGIVABLE!
WHAT THE ...?
...IRON TAIL!
WELL, IF I CAN'T STOP YOU, I'LL JUST HAVE TO STAB YOU WITH...
ZZZZ

GRAB
IT... STOPPED THE ATTACK?!
OOOMPH
SMASH

OW!
WHY...?
ZIP
YOU CAN'T
FIGURE OUT
WHY YOU
LOST?

POLI USED MIND READER BEFORE YOU ATTACKED ME WITH IRON TAIL...
GULP
MIND READER LETS POLI READ YOUR MOVES BEFORE YOU USE THEM, SO IT CAN PICK THE RIGHT ATTACK TO COUNTER THEM.

HOW COULD YOU DO SOMETHING SO AWFUL TO THIS ISLAND AND ALL THESE INNOCENT PEOPLE? THEY HAVE NOTHING TO DO WITH THIS!
I WON'T LET YOU DAMAGE THESE ISLANDS! WHY ARE YOU AFTER US ANYWAY?! IS IT BECAUSE WE'RE GETTING IN THE WAY OF YOUR SECRET PLAN?!
ANSWER ME!

NO. IT'S THE OTHER WAY AROUND.
?!
YOU'RE NOT IN OUR WAY.
AS A MATTER OF FACT, WE **NEED** YOU.
OUR ORDERS FROM GIOVANNI...
...ARE TO USE YOU TO LURE THE DNA POKÉMON DEOXYS TO US.
WE'VE BEEN INSTRUCTED TO CAPTURE YOU—AT ANY COST.

SIX ISLAND ...

SIGH ...

THIS IS SO-O-O BORING.

THE PEOPLE ON SIX ISLAND...

...ARE SO WEAK.

OW ...

URRGH ...

OOH, YOU DECIDED TO COME OUT! IMPRESSIVE!
CHARIZARD!
SRASH
FLAME-THROWER!

KRKL KRKL
TMP
?!
DON'T EXPECT TO SCORCH EVERYTHING THAT EASILY!
POP POP POP POP POP
YOUR FIRE-TYPE MOVES DON'T HAVE ANY EFFECT ON MY SHUCKLE WHEN THEY HIDE IN THEIR SHELLS.
POP POP POP
POP POP
AND ...

WRGGL
LUNGE
TOXIC!
SI
SI
NUTS!
ZZZ
ZZZ

SKRTCH SKRTCH
THESE LITTLE POKÉMON ARE CUTE ONCE YOU GET TO KNOW THEM.
MY MY... YOU DON'T SEEM TOO HAPPY ABOUT THIS.
ACK... URGH!
WRGGL
WE HAVE TO TAKE CARE OF OUR FAMILY, DON'T WE?
OUR FAMILY INCLUDES ALL KINDS OF POKÉ-MON.
WRGGL
OOH, AND ANOTHER THING! GIOVANNI TOLD ME THAT...
...THERE'S SOMEONE WHO'S AN IMPORTANT PART OF **YOUR** FAMILY TOO.
WOMMM
TAKE A LOOK AND SEE HOW HE'S DOING...
VRR
MBL

YOU'RE GOING TO USE US... TO LURE DEOXYS TO YOU?

BUT WHY US?

"DEOXYS AND THE POKÉDEX HOLDERS OF PALLET TOWN ATTRACT EACH OTHER.

"DEOXYS WILL APPEAR WHEREVER RED, BLUE AND GREEN ARE."

BILL SKIPPED SEVERAL GRADES AND GRADUATED AT AN UNUSUALLY YOUNG AGE FROM SEVERAL ACADEMIC INSTITUTIONS. HE IS HIGHLY INTELLIGENT AND WAS AT THE CENTER OF THE DEVELOPMENT OF THE POKÉMON STORAGE SYSTEM. HE CONDUCTS HIS RESEARCH AT A SEA COTTAGE ON CERULEAN CAPE WITH HIS ASSISTANT DAISY. HE IS CURRENTLY INVESTIGATING THE MYSTERY AT THE SEVII ISLANDS WITH RED AND THE OTHERS.

- Birthplace: Goldenrod City
- Birthday: December 31
- Blood Type: O
- Profession: Pokémon Storage System Developer & Manager, Pokémon Analyst, Pokémon Association Member.

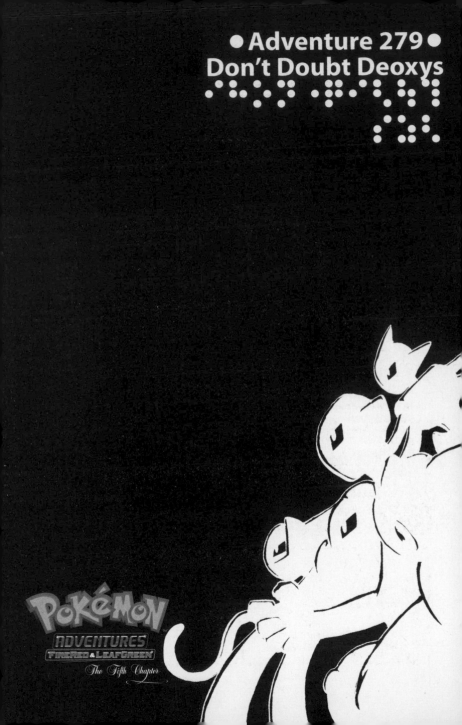

• Adventure 279 •
Don't Doubt Deoxys

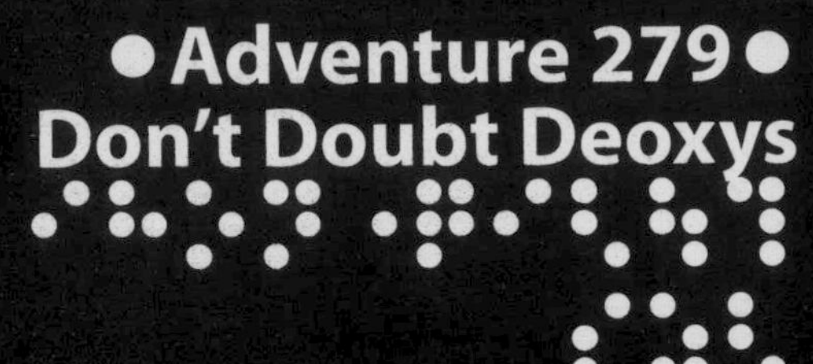

Pokémon Adventures
FireRed & LeafGreen
The Fifth Chapter

CITIZENS OF THE SEVII ISLANDS, IF YOU WANT US TO STOP THIS ATTACK, HAND OVER RED, BLUE AND GREEN OF PALLET TOWN!

ONE ISLAND...

POKÉMON NET CENTER...

THEY USED A POWERFUL ELECTROMAGNETIC WAVE TO HACK THE SEVII ISLANDS' TV BROADCAST NETWORK!

WANTED

THIS IMAGE IS BEING AIRED ALL OVER THE SEVII ISLANDS...

CELIO!
I'VE GOT TO CALL BILL AND TELL HIM RIGHT AWAY...
I'VE FINALLY FIGURED OUT...
...THE REASON THE POKÉMON TRANSPORTER WASN'T WORKING. IT'S BECAUSE THOSE GOONS WERE INTERRUPTING THE SIGNAL!
IT WAS ALL TEAM ROCKET'S FAULT!
HEY, I'VE FIGURED IT OUT! THE REASON THE POKÉMON TRANS-PORTER WAS—
NOW'S NOT THE TIME!

LOOK! FIVE ISLAND, SIX ISLAND AND SEVEN ISLAND...

THEY'RE ALL IN A TERRIBLE STATE DUE TO THE ATTACKS!

SEVII ISLAND WAS A PEACE-FUL PLACE UP TILL NOW!

WE KNOW THOSE THREE KIDS CAME TO THE POKÉMON NETWORK CENTER.

THEY'LL STOP THE ATTACK IF WE HAND THE KIDS OVER!

BRING THEM OUT!

RMBL

MUR MUR
MUR
I...
I HAVE TO... GO.
STGGR
STGGR

FIVE ISLAND...
THAT POKÉMON IS CALLED...
...DEOXYS.
AND DEOXYS AND THE POKÉDEX HOLDERS OF PALLET TOWN **ATTRACT** EACH OTHER SOMEHOW...
SO YOU'RE SAYING... **WE'RE** DRAWING THAT POKÉMON HERE?
IS THAT TRUE?!

I HAVE TO HELP THE VICTIMS OF THE ATTACK!
SAUR, DON'T LET HIM GO!
OW... SOMEBODY... HELP ME.
URRGH...
AHH!

ARE YOU OKAY...? I'VE CAPTURED THE GUY WHO WAS ATTACKING THIS ISLAND.
THERE'S NOTHING TO WORRY ABOUT.
LET GO OF ME!
SLAP
NOTHING TO WORRY ABOUT?!
ARE YOU KIDDING ME?!

I SAW THAT ANNOUNCEMENT, YOU KNOW!
YOU'RE THE REASON THE SEVII ISLANDS ARE BEING ATTACKED IN THE FIRST PLACE!
SO WHAT IF YOU STOPPED THE GUY WHO'S ATTACKING THIS ISLAND NOW?!
HIS TEAMMATES WILL KEEP TARGETING US AS LONG AS YOU'RE HERE!!
GRIN
UH...
HEY!
FLAP
FLAP
FLAP
WELL DONE, RED!
YOU'VE ALREADY CAPTURED SHORTY HERE, HUH?
RED?
THUNK
TMP

PLUS, RED IS A POKÉDEX HOLDER! PROFESSOR OAK, THE GREAT POKÉMON RESEARCHER, ENTRUSTED HIM WITH A POKÉDEX!

HE'S A **SPECIAL** TRAINER!

HEY! WHAT KIND OF THANKS IS THAT?!

RED CAME TO HELP Y'ALL! HE'S USED ALL HIS KNOWLEDGE AND TH' SKILLS HE'S HONED...

...TO FIGHT THE ENEMY!

OH YEAH? LET'S SEE THAT POKÉDEX THEN!
PROVE YOU'RE A SPECIAL TRAINER!
...

I... I...
...DON'T HAVE IT WITH ME RIGHT NOW, ACTUALLY...

SEE! HE BROUGHT ALL THIS DOWN ON US AND HE'S A LIAR TO BOOT!
WHAT'D YA SAY ?!
BILL!

IT'S OKAY.
DON'T.

RED ...

LUB DUB
WZZ ZZZ
BRRRR
?!
A POKÉMON WHO'S DRAWN TO THE POKÉDEX HOLDERS OF PALLET TOWN...
LUB
THE POKÉ-MON...
... DEOXYS.
DUB
WE... DRAW...
LUB DUB
...THAT POKÉMON... TO US!
LUB
DUB

WHAT'RE YOU TALKIN' 'BOUT, RED?!
BILL, I CAN'T EXPLAIN WHY, BUT...
... THERE'S ONE THING I KNOW FOR SURE!
IT'S HERE!
RMBL
IT WAS DRAWN TO ME!
ROOAAAR
AND NOW THAT POKÉ-MON ...
...HAS APPEARED!

YEEHAW!
IT'S HERE! IT'S HERE! IT'S HERE!
SO THIS IS DEOXYS ...
THE REAL ONE! I'VE NEVER MET THIS POKÉMON BEFORE!
THIS TRANSLUCENT VERSION ...
...IT'S THE ONE DITTO SAW ON THE SEAGALLOP.
SCRITCH
NO... IT'S CHANGED SHAPE!
IT'S TAKEN THE FORM OF THE POKÉMON WE SAW ON THE RECORDING ON THE SILPH SCOPE!

KRCK
WOM WOM WOM
OKAY, THUNDER-BOLT!
ZZZAAP
PIKA!

SHAT
IT CHANGED AGAIN!
INTO A DIFFERENT FORM!
GULP
FOOSH

M
B
L

IS THERE MORE THAN ONE ENEMY? IS THIS POKÉMON EVOLVING? OR MAYBE... THIS ENEMY CAN CHANGE SHAPES...
IT'S JUST LIKE BLUE THOUGHT!
THERE'S ONLY ONE ENEMY. BUT IT'S A UNIQUE POKÉMON WHO CHANGES ITS FORME DEPENDING ON THE SITUATION AND BATTLE-STYLE...

THAT'S RIGHT! IT'S CALLED ...
... FORME CHANGE!

FORME CHANGE ?!

WZZ ZZZZ

LET'S GO! PIKA! AERO!
FWIP FWIP
SWOOP
SWISH
ZZZZ
PLUNK
KLNCH

WOM WOM WOM
SHING
FWUMP

ITS TEN-
TACLES
CHANGED
SHAPE...
THEY'RE
SHARP
NOW!
SNAG
SWISH
AERO!

SNOR-!
SWING
SWING

SMASH

BACK AWAY, SNOR!

IT DIDN'T EVEN BUDGE?!

WOOO OO
HOW AM I SUPPOSED TO DEFEAT A POKÉMON THAT CAN FORME CHANGE?
IT KEEPS CHANG-ING!
...I'LL JUST HAVE TO DISCOVER ITS WEAK-NESSES ON MY OWN.
WELL... SINCE I DON'T, I GUESS...
IF ONLY I HAD MY POKÉ-DEX WITH ME...
PIKA!
FROM WHAT I'VE SEEN SO FAR, THE FORME WITH THE SHARP TENTACLES HAS A STRONG OFFENSE...
....AND THAT ROBUST LOOKING FORME HAS A STRONG DEFENSE!
GYARA!
BOOM
...I COULDN'T SEE IT CLEARLY.
I'M NOT SURE ABOUT THE FORME IT USED TO PUNCH US... THAT ONE WAS TRANS-LUCENT, SO...

THE DEFENSIVE SHAPE IS CALLED THE DEFENSE FORME.
ALLOW ME TO OFFER YOU SOME TERMS FOR YOUR OBSERVATIONS...
THE OFFENSIVE SHAPE IS CALLED THE ATTACK FORME.
OOH! YOU'RE QUITE THE OBSERVANT ONE!
AND YOU'RE RIGHT SO FAR.
OOH!
386 Deoxys
DNA Pokémon
Height: 5'07"
Weight: 134.0lbs.
When it changes form, an aurora appears. It absorbs attacks by altering its cellular structure.
OH!
No. 386 Deoxys
DNA Pokémon
Height: 5'07"
Weight: 134.0lbs.
This Deoxys has transformed into its aggressive guise. It can fool enemies by altering its appearance.
AND THE DATA I GATHERED FROM SEEING IT IN ACTION NEARBY IS...
IT'S BLACK, BUT IT LOOKS AND FUNCTIONS...
THAT DEVICE...
HEH HEH HEH! THIS IS WONDERFUL.
IT'S CLEAR THAT IT SURPASSES ANY ORDINARY POKÉMON!
...JUST LIKE A POKÉDEX!
BOING
BOING

AFTER ALL, THAT CAN'T BE THE ONLY SECRET...
...OF ITS FORME CHANGES.

LA LA LA... I MUST STUDY THIS POKÉMON MORE.

HEY! THAT MACHINE ...!
WHERE'D YA GET THAT THING?!

RED AND BLUE SAID...

...PROFESSOR OAK UP AND DISAPPEARED... LEAVIN' BEHIND A MESSAGE FOR THEM TA GIVE UP THEIR POKÉDEXES. THAT'S WHEN THIS WHOLE SHEBANG STARTED...

OOPSY-DAISY!
WHY YOU ...!

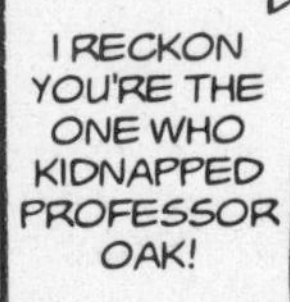
I RECKON YOU'RE THE ONE WHO KIDNAPPED PROFESSOR OAK!

IT WAS YOU, WASN'T IT?!

THAT'S RIGHT.
WE, THE THREE BEASTS OF TEAM ROCKET...
...HAVE KIDNAPPED PROFES-SOR OAK.

MACHAMP! SCIZOR!

I DON'T CARE IF YOU HIT US TOO! USE EVERYTHING YOU'VE GOT TO TEAR THESE SHUCKLE OFF OF US!

YEP. AND YOU CAN'T DO A THING ABOUT IT.

YOU KID-NAPPED MY GRAND-FATHER!

METAL CLAW!

GLARE

FOOSH

HYPER BEAM!

HEH HEH HEH HEH HEH.

WHOA!

THUNK

URGH!

KRASH

I GUESS THE LOVE OF FAMILY IS A POWER-FUL EMOTION.

I'LL ADMIT, HE'S GOT GUTS.

FZZZZZZ
THERE THERE, CUTE LITTLE SHUCKLE. WHO'S A CUTE SHUCKLE, HM...?
WE'LL GO FOR A STROLL IN A FIELD OF FLOWERS AFTER THIS IS ALL OVER.
PAT PAT
BUT BONDS BETWEEN SHUCKLE ARE STRONG TOO.
OW!
WHAT WAS THAT?!
A DRILL ?!
WZ ZZZT
IT'S IMPOSSIBLE FOR YA TO GIVE ORDERS T' EVERY SINGLE ONE OF THOSE POKÉMON!
WHICH MEANS THE SHUCKLE ON YOUR TEAM MUST BE IN COMMAND OF ALL THOSE OTHER WILD SHUCKLE!
KE DRRAK
ALL I HAFTA DO TO DEFEAT YOUR SHUCKLE IS TO DISRUPT THE UNITY OF THE OTHERS!

FWUMP

PFFF

SWASH

YOU CAN TAKE THAT STROLL LATER IN YOUR DREAMS!

...BUT YOU DIDN'T NOTICE.
SCIZOR AND MACHAMP'S ATTACK WAS DESIGNED TO LURE YOU RIGHT ABOVE MY RHYDON...

WHERE ARE YOU...?

AHH! SIX ISLAND AND SEVEN ISLAND ARE IN CHAOS TOO NOW...

I HOPE RED, BLUE AND THAT GIRL WITH THE GLASSES ARE OKAY...
RING
HUH ?

IT'S ME!
ULTIMA?! I-IS THERE SOME-THING I CAN DO FOR YOU?
Ack.

YES, THAT'S WHY I'M CALL-ING!
COME AND PICK ME UP WITH THE SEAGALLOP RIGHT AWAY!
I'M GOING TO ONE ISLAND!
WHAT?! WHY?!

DON'T WASTETIME JIBBER-JABBERING! HOP TO IT! ON THE DOUBLE!
AIYEEE!

...
KLNK

LTIMA ...!

WE'RE LIKE BEGINNERS WHEN IT COMES TO WIELDING YOUR SPECIAL MOVES... BUT I GOT THE GRASS-TYPE MOVE, FRENZY PLANT...
...AND BLUE GOT THE FIRE-TYPE SPECIAL MOVE, BLAST BURN.
THAT'S RIGHT.

THIS IS JUST A WILD GUESS, BUT...I'M THINKING THE REMAINING RING...

...INSIDE THAT BRACELET...
...IS A WATER-TYPE MOVE.

AM I RIGHT?
WHY DO YOU WANT TO KNOW?

DITTO SHOWED YOU WHAT HAPPENED ON THE *SEAGALLOP*. IT'S SIMPLE...

THERE'S A GIRL NAMED GREEN WHO CAME WITH US TO THE SEVII ISLANDS.
SHE'S A SKILLED TRAINER WHO USES A BLASTOISE.

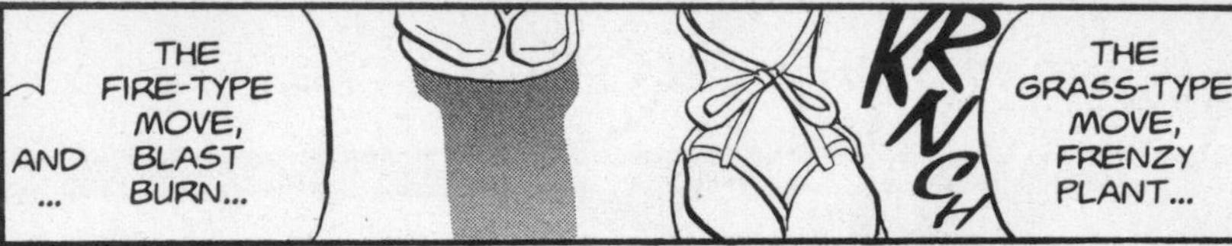

...THE WATER-TYPE MOVE, HYDRO CANNON...

TINGLE

WOOO
THREE TRAINERS WORTHY OF LEARN-ING THESE MOVES APPEARED AT THE SAME TIME. I NEVER THOUGHT I'D LIVE TO SEE THE DAY!
THIS MUST MEAN THAT... THE WHEELS OF FATE... ARE BEGINNING TO TURN.

LOOK, PIKA! A CLOUD IS COVER-ING THE SKY.

RMBLRMB

CAN YOU DO IT...?

GO! THUNDER!
FLASH

TRMBL TRMBL

YEAH! YOU DID IT, PIKA!
SEEMS LIKE THE CRYSTAL IN ITS CHEST IS THE SOURCE OF ITS POWER!

IT LOOKS LIKE IT CAN'T CHANGE FORMES AGAIN NOW!

WZZZZ

IT'S REGAIN-ING ITS POWER AGAIN!

OOH! RECOVER!

HEF HEF

WEF WEF

PIKA, USE THUNDER AGAIN! STRIKE ITS CRYSTAL!

WEF

I SEE YOUR PIKACHU CAN'T USE THUNDER ANYMORE...

...THANKS TO DEOXYS'S ABILITY PRESSURE.

THIS IS IT! DEOXYS'S GREATEST MOVE...
OOOH! POWER OF 140!
...PSYCHO BOOST!
STUDY COMPLETE...
FMP
TO BE CONTINUED...

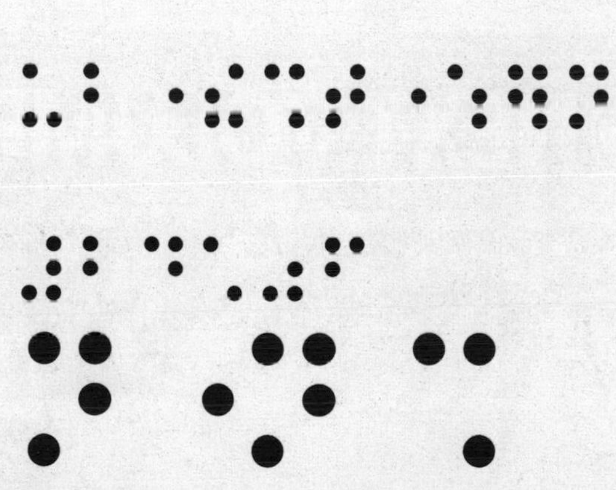

WE WEREN'T STRONG ENOUGH.

...LOST.

THE DNA POKÉMON, DEOXYS!

RED IS CRUSHED BY ITS OVERWHELMING POWER!

NEXT VOLUME!

THE DEFEAT...

...LEADS TO STRIFE!

WHAT ...?!
THAT'S EASY FOR YOU TO SAY, BECAUSE YOU DIDN'T FIGHT IT!
SHOVE
CONFIDENCE, PRIDE, FRIENDSHIP— ALL THREE ARE ON THE LINE!
WHAT ?!
YAK
WILL EVERYTHING THEY'VE BUILT UP TOGETHER FALL APART?
MAYBE ...
...THIS IS WHY PROFES-SOR OAK TOOK THE POKÉDEX AWAYFROM ME...
!
AS RED STRUGGLES, WHO SHOULD APPEAR BEFORE HIM BUT...?
POKÉMON ADVENTURES Volume 24!
RED ...
THE EMOTION YOU CARRY INSIDE YOU... I UNDER-STAND IT WELL.
WILL RED GET BACK ON HIS FEET...?!

Message from
Hidenori Kusaka

Adventure 268, "The Escape," (included in this volume) is an episode we created for a grade school magazine. At the time, we didn't plan to include it in the graphic novel, and that's what we told our readers. But we kept getting requests from fans who didn't get to read it in the magazine asking us to include it in the graphic novel. So we decided to go ahead and do it. I'm always astounded by the passionate support of our readers! And now, please sit back, relax and enjoy this volume!

Message from
Satoshi Yamamoto

The Fifth Chapter of *Pokémon Adventures* starts in this volume. Red and Blue return to their hometown, only to depart again because of the appearance of a new enemy. This journey will be tougher than anything they have experienced before! Red and the others seem to have mastered their skills as Pokémon Trainers, but now you'll see how they take on the new challenge before them.

More Adventures Coming Soon...

Red is downhearted after being defeated by the Legendary Pokémon Deoxys and fears that Professor Oak has given up on him. With the support of Blue and Green and an unexpected powerful Pokémon ally, he continues on his journey. But then he must face a formidable human opponent—Giovanni!

Meanwhile, what clues to his past will Silver find in Viridian City...?

AVAILABLE
SEPTEMBER
2014!

PERFECT SQUARE
POKÉMON
ADVENTURES
FIRERED & LEAFGREEN
TM
24
VOLUME TWENTY-FOUR
Story by Hidenori Kusaka
Art by Satoshi Yamamoto

POKÉMON™ BLACK & WHITE

STORY & ART BY SANTA HARUKAZE

YOUR FAVORITE POKEMON FROM THE UNOVA REGION LIKE YOU'VE NEVER SEEN THEM BEFORE!

Available now!

A pocket-sized book brick jam-packed with four-panel comic strips featuring all the Pokémon Black and White characters, Pokémon vital statistics, trivia, puzzles, and fun quizzes!

www.viz.com

ratings.viz.com